# THE
# STANDING
# CHANDELIER

## ALSO BY LIONEL SHRIVER

*The Mandibles: A Family, 2029 – 2047*

*Big Brother*

*The New Republic*

*So Much for That*

*The Post-Birthday World*

*We Need to Talk About Kevin*

*Double Fault*

*A Perfectly Good Family*

*Game Control*

*Ordinary Decent Criminals*

*Checker and the Derailleurs*

*The Female of the Species*

# THE
# STANDING
# CHANDELIER

## LIONEL
## SHRIVER

THE BOROUGH PRESS

The Borough Press
An imprint of HarperCollins*Publishers*
1 London Bridge Street
London SE1 9GF

www.harpercollins.co.uk

Published by HarperCollins*Publishers* 2017
1

Copyright © Lionel Shriver 2017

Lionel Shriver asserts the moral right to be identified as the author of this work

A catalogue record for this book is available from the British Library

HB ISBN: 978-0-00-826527-4

Set in Adobe Garamond 12/18 pt by Palimpsest Book Production Limited,
Falkirk, Stirlingshire

Printed and bound in Great Britain by CPI Group (UK) Ltd, Croydon, CR0 4YY

MIX
Paper from
responsible sources
FSC
www.fsc.org FSC™ C007454

This book is produced from independently certified FSC™ paper
to ensure responsible forest management.

For more information visit: www.harpercollins.co.uk/green

*In bottomless gratitude, to Jeff and Sue.*
*This is not about you.*

J illian Frisk found the experience of being disliked bewildering. Or not bewildering enough, come to think of it, since the temptation was always to see her detractor's point of view. Newly aware of a woman's aversion—it was always another woman, and perhaps that meant something, something in itself not very nice—she would feel awkward, at a loss, mystified, even a little frightened. Paralyzed. In a traducer's presence, she'd yearn to refute whatever about herself was purportedly so detestable. Yet no matter what she said, or what she did, she would involuntarily verify the very qualities that the faultfinder couldn't bear. Vanity? Flakiness? Staginess?

For an intrinsic facet of being disliked was racking your brain for whatever it was that rubbed other people so radically the wrong way. They rarely told you to your face, so you were left with a burgeoning list of obnoxious characteristics that *you compiled for them*. So Jillian would demote her garb from *festive* to *garish* or even *vulgar*, and suddenly see how her offbeat thrift shop ensembles, replete with velvet

1

vests, broad belts, tiered skirts, and enough scarves to kill Isadora Duncan three times over, could seem to demonstrate *attention-seeking behavior*. A clear, forceful voice was to the leery merely *loud*, and whenever she suppressed the volume the better to give no offense, she simply became inaudible, which was maddening, too. Besides, she didn't seem capable of maintaining a mousy, head-down demeanor for more than half an hour, during which the sensation was tantamount to a Chinese foot binding of the soul. Wide gesticulation when she grew exuberant was doubtless *histrionic*. Smitten by another smoldering black look from across a table, she would sometimes trap her hands in her lap, where they would flap like captured birds. But in a moment of inattention, the dratted extremities always escaped, flinging her napkin to the floor. Her full-throated guffaw would echo in her own ears as *an annoying laugh*. (Whatever did you do about an annoying laugh? Stop finding anything funny?) Then on top of all the ghastly attributes she embodied, merely being in the presence of someone who she knew couldn't stand her slathered on an additionally off-putting surface of nervousness, contrition, and can't-beat-them-join-them self-suspicion.

But then, Jillian should have known better by now, having enough times withstood the gamut from distaste to loathing (yet rarely indifference). When people didn't like you, if this doesn't seem too obvious, they didn't like *you*. That is, the problem wasn't an identifiable set of habits, beliefs, and traits—say, a propensity for leaning against a counter with a jauntily jutted hip as if you thought you were hot stuff, overusage of the word *fabulous*, a misguided conviction that refusing to vote is making a political statement, a tendency to mug the more premeditative with a sudden impulse to go camping this very afternoon and to make them feel like spoilsports when they didn't want to go. No, it was the sum total that rankled, the whole package, the essence from which all of these evidences sprang. Jillian could remain perfectly still with her mouth zipped, and Estelle Pettiford—a fellow crafts counselor at the Maryland summer camp where Jillian worked for a couple of seasons, whose idea of compelling recreation for fifteen-year-olds was making Christmas trees out of phone books in July—would still have hated her, and the girl would have kept hating her even if this object of odium didn't move a muscle or utter a syllable through to the end of time. That was what slew Jillian about being disliked: There was no remedy, no chance of tempering an antipathy into, say, forbearance or healthy apathy. It was simply your being in the world that drove these people insane, and even if you killed yourself, your suicide would annoy them, too. More *attention seeking*.

Glib, standard advice would be not to care. Right. Except

that shrugging off the fact that someone despised you was impossible. The expectation was inhuman, so that, on top of having someone hate you, you cared that someone hated you and apparently you shouldn't. Caring made you even more hateable. Your inability to dismiss another's animus was one more thing that was wrong with you. Because that was the thing: these sneering, disgusted perceptions always seemed to have more clout than the affections of all the other people who thought you were delightful. Your friends had been duped. The naysayers had your number.

There was Linda Warburton, her coworker during a stint leading tours at the Stonewall Jackson House, who grew insensibly enraged every time Jillian brewed strong coffee in the staff kitchen—Jillian made strong everything—as the girl preferred her java weak. After Jillian began going to the extra trouble of boiling a kettle so that Linda could dilute her own mug to her heart's content, the accommodation to everyone's tastes seemed only to drive the lumpy, prematurely middle-aged twenty-five-year-old to more ferocious abhorrence: Linda actually submitted a formal complaint to the Virginia Tourist Board that Jillian Frisk wore the bonnet of her costume at "an historically inaccurate cocky slant." There was Tatum O'Hagan, the clingy, misbegotten roommate of 1998, who'd seemed to want to become bosom buddies when Jillian first moved in—in fact, the brownie-baking sharing of confidences became a bit much—but who, once Jillian inserted a merciful crack of daylight between the two, came to find her presence so unendurable that she posted a roster of which evenings one or the other could occupy the living room and which hours—different hours—they could cook. There was the officious Olivia Auerbach only two years ago, another unpaid organizer of the annual Maury River Fiddlers Convention, who accused her of "distracting the musicians from their practice" and "overstepping the necessarily humble role of a volunteer." (And how. Jillian had a sizzling affair with a participant from Tennessee, who knew how to fiddle with more than his bow.)

Tall and slender, with a thick thatch of kinked henna hair that tumbled to her elbows, Jillian had trouble being inconspicuous, and that wasn't her fault. She supposed she was pretty, though that adjective seemed to have a statute of limitations attached. At forty-three, she'd probably been downgraded to *attractive*—in preparation, since postmenopausal flattery went unisex, for *handsome*; gosh, she could hardly wait for *well preserved.* So she might plausibly dismiss this bafflingly consistent incidence of female animosity as bitchy takedown in a catwalk competition. But when she glanced around Lexington, which flushed every fall with an influx of fetching freshmen from Washington and Lee—

whose appearance of getting younger each year helped track her own decay—Jillian was often awed by the profusion of beautiful women in the world, not all of whom could have been unrelenting targets of antagonism. To the contrary, in her high school days in Pittsburgh, when Jillian was gawky and still uncomfortable with her height, students flocked to sunny blond bombshells, who often benefited from a reputation for kindness and generosity purely for bestowing the occasional smile. Her problem wasn't looks, or looks alone, even if the hair in particular seemed to make a declaration that she didn't intend. Jillian had hair that you had to live up to.

So looking back, it had been naive in the extreme to have innocently posted photographs of various homespun creations in the early days of social media, in anticipation of a few anodyne responses like, "Cute!" or "Super!"—or in anticipation of no response, which would have been fine, too. When instead her set of handmade dishware attracted, "You're a talentless, amateur hack" and "Suggest trampling these misshapen atrocities into landfill," Jillian drew back as if having put a hand on a hot stove. By the time that comments on such applications escalated to routine rape threats, she had long since canceled her accounts.

It did seem to irk some sorts that Jillian was a self-confessed dabbler. She taught herself a sprinkling of Italian, for example, but in a spirit of frivolity, and not because she planned to visit Rome but because she liked the sound—the expressive *mama mia* up and down of it, the popping carbonation it imparted even to *little pencil*: "picolla matita." Yet the phase was to no purpose, and that was the point. Jillian pursued purposelessness as a purpose in itself. It had taken her some years to understand that she'd had such trouble settling on a career because she didn't want one. She was surrounded by go-getters, and they could have their goals, their trajectories, their aspirations—their feverish toiling toward some distant destination that was bound to disappoint in the unlikely instance they ever got there. Some folks had to savor the world where they were, as opposed to glancing out the driver's window while tearing off somewhere else. This was less a prescriptive ideology than a simple inclination to languor or even laziness; Jillian cheerfully accepted that. She wasn't so much out to convert anyone else as to simply stop apologizing.

It was curious how furious it made some people that you didn't want to "make something of yourself" when you were something already and had no particular desire to change, or that you could declare beamingly that you were "altogether aimless" in a tone of voice that implied this was nothing to be ashamed of. Jillian had recently been informed at the bar of Bistro on Main that, for an expensively educated woman with a better-than-middle-class background who enjoyed ample "opportunities," having no especial objective aside from enjoying herself was "un-American."

Jillian had the kind of charm that wore off. Or after enough romantic diminuendos, that's what she theorized. Even for guys, whose gender seemed to preclude the full-fledged anaphylactic shock of an allergic reaction, the profusion of her playful little projects, which were never intended to make a name, or get a gallery, or attract a review in the *Roanoke Times*, might appear diverting and even a measure entrancing at first, but eventually she'd seem childish, or bats, or embarrassing, and men moved on.

With one crucial exception.

She'd met Weston Babansky while taking a poorly taught English course when they were both undergraduates at Washington and Lee. Their instructor was disorganized, with a tendency to mutter, so that you couldn't tell when he was addressing the seminar or talking to himself. She'd been impressed by the fact that after class Weston—or "Baba," as she christened him after they'd grown to know each other better—was reluctant to bandwagon about Steve Reardon's execrable lectures with the other students, who railed about paying tuition through the nose for this rambling, incoherent mishmash with a relish that alone explained why they didn't transfer out. Instead Baba was sympathetic. The first time they had coffee, he told Jillian that actually, if you listened closely, a lot of what Reardon said was pretty interesting. The trouble was that qualifying as an academic didn't mean you were a performer, and teaching was theater. He said he himself didn't imagine he'd be any better up there, and on that score he was probably right. Weston Babansky was inward, reflective, avoidant of the spotlight.

Already subjected to multiple aversions, Jillian appreciated his sensitivity—although there was nothing soft or effeminate about the man, who was three or four years older than most of their classmates. No sooner did he express an opinion than he immediately experienced what it was like on its receiving end, as if firing a Wile E. Coyote rifle whose barrel was U-shaped. It was one of the many topics the two had teased out since: how careless people were with their antipathy, how they threw it around for fun; how these days people indiscriminately sprayed vituperation every which way as if launching a mass acid attack in a crowded public square. Sheer meanness had become a customary form of entertainment. Since the disapprobation she'd drawn that she knew about was doubtless dwarfed by the mountain of behind-the-back ridicule that she didn't, Jillian herself had grown ever more reluctant to contrive a dislike even for celebrities who would never know the difference—pop stars, politicians, actors, or news anchors, whose high public profile presumably made them fair game. She'd catch herself saying, "Oh, I can't stand him," then immediately hear the denunciation with the victim's ears, and wince.

It turned out that Baba was also a northerner, and in respect to his future, equally at sea. Best of all, they were each on the lookout for a tennis partner—ideally one who wouldn't scornfully write you off the moment a wild forehand flew over the fence.

Lo, from their first hit they were perfectly suited. They both took a long time to warm up, and appreciated wit as well as power. They both preferred rallying for hours on end to formal games; they still played proper points, which would be won or lost, but no one kept score—more of Jillian's purposive purposelessness. It didn't hurt that Baba was handsome, though in that bashful way that most people overlooked, with the stringy, loose-jointed limbs of a natural tennis player. He was ferocious, hard hitting, and nefarious on court, but the killer instinct evaporated the moment he exited the chain-link gate. His tendency to grow enraged with himself over unforced errors was Jillian's secret weapon. After three or four of his backhands in a row smacked the tape, he did all the hard work for her: he would defeat himself. He was complicated, more so than others seemed to recognize, with a dragging propensity for depression to which he admitted as a generality, but never actively inflicted on present company.

She also found his understated social unease more endearing than the facility of raconteurs and bons vivants who greased the skids at parties by never running out of things to say. Baba often ran out of things to say, in which case he said nothing. She learned from him that silence needn't be mortifying, and some of their most luxuriant time together was quiet.

Baba was something of a recluse, who kept odd hours and did his best work at four a.m.; Jillian had joked that if the courts had lights, she'd never get a point off him. She was the more gregarious of the two, so after they'd exhausted themselves bashing balls back and forth it was Jillian who delivered the bulk of the stories for their ritual debrief on a courtside bench. For a man, he was unusually fascinated with teasing out fine filaments of feeling. Thus they used each other as sounding boards about the friends and lovers who came and went. Baba was neither perturbed nor surprised when one of the seniors in Jillian's dormitory suite came to so revile her company that the moment Jillian entered the suite's common area the girl flounced back to her room. "You have a strong flavor," he said. "Some people just don't like anchovies."

"Liver," Jillian corrected with a laugh. "When I walk in, she acts more like someone slid her an enormous slab of offal—overcooked, grainy, and reeking."

In fact, which badinage proved the more engaging was a toss-up: the assertion and reply on court, or the tête-à-tête when they were through. One conversation seemed a continuation of the other by different means. As a walloping approach shot could be followed by a dink, Baba would no sooner have questioned on the bench whether it was really worth his while to complete his degree at William and Lee (the interest he was rounding on was computer networks, a field transforming so quickly that most of what he was studying was out of date) than Jillian would mention having discovered a great five-minute recipe for parmesan chicken. The conversational ball skittered across all four corners of their lives, from lofty speculative lobs about how, if energy was neither created nor destroyed, could that mean there was necessarily life after death—or even life before life?—to single put-aways about how *Jerry Springer* had a campy appeal at first, but ultimately was unendurable. It was with Baba that Jillian first began to haltingly explore that maybe she didn't want to "be" something she wasn't already, and with whom she initially considered the possibility of making things outside the confines of the pompous, overwhelmingly bogus art world. Together they agreed on the importance of owning their own lives, and their own time; they viewed the nine-to-five slog of a wage earner with a mutual shudder.

Jillian finally settled on a suitably diffuse degree on cross-fertilization in the arts (which got her adulthood off to a thematically pertinent start by serving no earthly purpose) while Baba's major had more of a science bent (she could no longer remember what it was)—she loitered in Lexington, tutoring lagging local high schoolers in grammar, vocabulary, and math, often for SAT prep. That was the mid-1990s, when the internet was taking off, and as a freelance website designer Baba easily snagged as much work as he cared to handle. So from the start, they both did jobs you could do from anywhere.

But if you could be anywhere, you could also stay put. Lexington was a pleasant college town, with distinguished colonial architecture and energizing infusions of tourists and Civil War buffs. Virginia weather was clement, spring through fall. And what mattered, other than Jillian's point-less, peculiar projects—the hand-sewn drapes with hokey tassels, the collage of quirky headlines ("Woman Sues for Being Born")—was being able to play tennis with your ideal partner three times a week.

Tired of having to defer to the teams, the two retired from the college courts where they might have continued to play as alumnae, preferring the three funky, more concealed public courts at Rockbridge County High School, which were sheltered by a bank of tall trees and blighted with just enough cracks to add an element of chance (or better, something to blame). Especially summers, they'd retire to the bench and muse for an hour or two, while the humid southern air packed around them like pillows. Jillian would ruffle the crystallized sweat on her arms and sometimes lick it, having become, as she said, "a human Dorito." They still shared recipes and disparaged television programs, but their mainstay was the mysteries of other people.

"Okay, I know I said I wouldn't, but you predicted it, and you were right," Jillian once introduced. "I slept with Sullivan on Friday. Now, it wasn't terrible or anything, but get this: in the throes of, ah, the thing itself, he starts announcing, full voice, 'I'm so aroused!' Over and over, 'I'm so *aroused.*' Now, who says that?"

"People say all kinds of things during sex," Baba allowed. "You ought to be able to say whatever you want. Maybe you should be a little easier on the guy."

"I'm not criticizing exactly. But still, it's so abstracted. Removed. Like he was watching himself, or . . . I mean, most people get off on stuff that goes back to puberty or even earlier, and 'I'm so aroused' sounds so hyperadult. Stiff and formal and almost third person. *I'm so aroused*? Tell me that's normal."

"There is no normal."

"But you can't imagine how *unarousing* it is to be officially informed that your partner is 'aroused.' Though at least Sullivan's swooning beat Andrew Carver's. That guy kept crooning, 'Oooh, baby! Oooh, baby, baby, baby!' Made my skin crawl."

"That's it," Baba announced. "I'm not sleeping with you, Frisk, if you have to have script approval."

That was a vow he would break. Perhaps tragically at different junctures, each fell in love with the other—abruptly, hard, all in. The first go-round, Baba had a steady girlfriend, and they conducted a torrid affair on the side until, feeling guilty over the disloyalty to his main squeeze, he reluctantly called it off. During their reprise—two, three, four years later? The chronology had grown hazy now—Jillian misinterpreted their reinvolvement as the idle entertainment of what were then called *fuck buddies* and later *friends with benefits*. So when she had a weekend fling with a dashing bartender, she naturally told Baba all about it after tennis. He was literally struck dumb—collapsing so inertly onto their regular bench that it was a wonder he was not still slumped there to this day.

In this one-two punch, which of the two had suffered more grievously was a matter of some dispute, and after both sexual terminations there ensued an agonizing interregnum during which they didn't talk or, worse, play tennis. Jillian would never forget migrating on her lonesome to their regular after-hit bench, kneeling on the ground, and resting her forehead on the rough, paint-peeling front slat in a position that could only have been called prayerful. And then she wailed, that was the word for it, and the cries emitted from the very center of her diaphragm, the part of the body from which one is taught to sing in opera. The theater would have been melodramatic had anyone been watching, but at least to begin with she was by herself. Until a teacher rushed to the parking lot and shouted, "Are you all right?" He must have thought she was being attacked—which in a way she was. Intriguingly, she could no longer recollect whether she made that pilgrimage in the aftermath of being rejected or doing the rejecting, for it was a hard call which role had been the more awful.

Weston Babansky and Jillian Frisk were best friends—a relationship cheapened by an expression like *BFF*, which notoriously referenced a companion to whom you wouldn't be speaking by next week. They had known each other for twenty-four years, and never in all that time had an interloper laid claim to the superlative. That exercise in mutual devastation was inoculating, and raised the relationship to what at least felt like a higher spiritual plane. Post-romance, post-sex, neither was tortured with curiosity about the twining of each other's limbs. Baba wasn't circumcised; Jillian refused to shave her bikini line: their secrets were out. It was a certain bet that, having survived the worst, they really would be *best friends forever*, thereby proving to the rest of the world that there was such a thing.

The millennium onward, Jillian had lived in a sweet, self-sufficient outbuilding of an antebellum estate, which she kept an eye on when the owners were abroad. She lived rent-free, and received a modest stipend in addition for receiving packages, retrieving the mail, taking trash cans to the curb and back, watering the potted plants in the main house, holding the gate open for the gardener, and agreeing not to take overnight trips if the Chevaliers were away. It was a cushy situation that all those aspirants desperate to be film directors might have seen as a trap. But the four-room cottage was just big enough to accommodate flurries of industry—the melees of crepe paper, plywood, rubber cement, and carpet tacks when Jillian plunged into another purposeless *project*. She'd been given free rein to redecorate, so refinishing the oak flooring, stitching tablecloths, tiling the bathroom, stripping tables, and repairing rickety rocking chairs kept her agreeably occupied when more elaborate creations weren't commanding her attention. A few years back, Baba had finally bought a house, like a good grown-up—an unconventional A-frame whose rough-hewn, homemade quality always reminded her of a tree house—but Jillian enjoyed all the advantages of a homeowner, as far as she could see, without the grief.

Patching together the stipend and a variety of odd jobs, Jillian approached earning her keep like quilting. She continued to tutor, in addition to subbing at Rockbridge County High School, so long as the gig didn't involve supervising any after-school activities on Mondays, Wednesdays, or Fridays, her regular tennis days. She got on well with children; if nothing else, they seemed always to love her hair. Having youngsters in her orbit took the sting out of the fact that it was looking as if she'd never have a family of her own. Having had plenty of exposure, she wasn't sentimental about kids, and often suspected their parents were a little envious that when her lessons were done she got to go home alone.

About the absence of a lover who stuck around, she was more wistful. Yet the urgency of finding a lifelong soul mate that had infused her twenties and thirties had given way to a state far more agreeable than some sullen resignation. She was still open. She had not given up. But she would rather be on her own than go through yet another roller-coaster ride of mounting intoxication and plummeting heartache. She had a rich life, with a smattering of interesting friends. She had tennis, and she had Baba.

Who had himself run through a surprisingly large population of women. Contrary to type—the subtle misfit, the mild sociophobe, the loner who might be expected to fall hopelessly head over heels once his defenses dropped—Baba had ended nearly all these relationships himself. The very ear for individual notes in an emotional chord that Jillian found so captivating meant that one or more of those notes, for Baba, was always a touch off-key. We are all audiences of our own lives, and in listening to the symphony of his feelings, Baba was like one of those musical prodigies who could detect one missing accidental—B flat, not B natural—in the fifth chair of the viola section, ruining the whole piece for him, while less attentive concertgoers would find the performance tuneful.

Yet for the last couple of years, a duration unheard of, he'd been seeing a somewhat younger woman who worked in admissions at William and Lee, and a year ago—another first—Paige Myer had moved into his house.

Jillian wasn't precisely jealous; on second thought, not at all jealous. When he started seeing Paige, Weston Babansky was already forty-five, and a lasting attachment was overdue. Jillian loved Baba in a round, encompassing, roomy way, and if she still found him technically attractive, the sensation was purely aesthetic. She enjoyed being in his physical company the way she enjoyed sitting in a smartly decorated restaurant. This pleasing feeling didn't induce any need to do something about it, any more than she ever experienced the urge to fuck a dining room.

So far, only once had Paige Myer's entry into Baba's life caused Jillian genuine alarm. It was a fall afternoon, on their usual bench at Rockbridge, a few months into this new relationship.

"By the way," he introduced. "I've been teaching Paige to play tennis."

Jillian narrowed her eyes and glared. "You're trying to replace me."

He laughed. "You're such a baby!"

"On this point, yes."

"You and I aren't exclusive, you know. We both sometimes play with other people. Sport is promiscuous."

"There's having a bit on the side, there's being a whore, and there's also throwing over an old, predictable partner for sexier fresh meat. *And* there are only so many days in the week. Why wouldn't my three afternoons seem imperiled?"

He was enjoying this. It was the kind of jealousy in which one could bask, and he brought it to a close with obvious regret. "Well, you can relax. The tennis lessons have been a disaster."

Jillian leaped up and did a little dance. "Yay!"

"It isn't becoming to take that much joy in another woman's suffering," he admonished.

"I don't care whether it's *becoming*. I care about nailing down my Monday, Wednesday, and Friday slots." She sat back down with zest. "Tell me all about it."

"I made her cry."

"You didn't."

"It's just—it would take years to narrow the skills gap. She's a complete newbie, and she wasn't doing it because she especially wanted to play tennis. She just wanted to do something with me—and in that case, we're better off going to the movies. I'm not sure she has much aptitude, and I definitely don't have the patience. The boredom was claustrophobic. I don't know how the pros can stand it. I had to call a halt to the lessons, because if we kept torturing ourselves we were going to split up. She made me feel like a tyrant, and I made her feel inadequate."

"Did you two come here?" Jillian asked warily.

"No, I took her to the university courts."

"Good. Rockbridge would have been traitorous."

"The guys next to us, the last time we went on this fool's errand—Paige sent so many balls into their court that they started smashing them back two courts over. You'd have loved it, you ill-wishing bitch," he said fondly.

"I'd have loved it," she concurred. "Except I'm *not* ill wishing. At least so long as she stays off my fucking tennis court."

Admittedly, the first time they all met could have gone better. Inviting Jillian to dinner sometime that January, Baba had been unusually anxious about the introduction, her first intimation that this relationship was hitting a harmonious major chord. Getting ready that night, Jillian considered that it might have been politic to bunch back the hair into a less in-your-face look, but she hadn't timed her shower well, and the tresses were still damp. Going back and forth over what to wear, she worried that plain jeans would seem disrespectful of the occasion, so she went the opposite direction. In retrospect, the fawn-colored boa was a mistake, even if the finishing flourish had presented itself as irresistible in her bedroom mirror. But it wasn't the boa that got her into trouble.

When she first burst into Baba's kitchen, she realized she must have been anxious, too, since in the flurry of delivering the wine and divesting herself of the tiny present wrapped in birch bark, she forgot to really take in the new girlfriend—what she looked like, how she seemed. Although nearly as at home in Baba's A-frame as she was in her own cottage, Jillian was officially the guest. Thus she naturally got confused at first about whose job it was to put whom at ease. "I've been doing a little beadwork, see," she babbled with her coat still on, nodding at the package. "You can find all kinds of wild costume jewelry from yard sales, thrift shops, whole boxes of the stuff on eBay . . . Anyway, you get a lot more interesting effects when you break up the strings and mix the elements in different combinations . . ."

One didn't exactly unwrap birch bark, and the gratuity simply fell out of the fragile assemblage into Paige's palm. In her hand, suddenly the necklace looked a little cockamamie. "Oh," she said. "How nice."

"I'm still experimenting," Jillian carried on, "throwing in other found materials, like pinecone, gum-wrapper origami, pieces of eraser, even dead batteries . . ."

Paige's gaze scanned slowly back up. "Don't you think," she said, "that after all the progress we've finally made on animal rights, it might not be wise to be seen in public wearing a fur?"

Jillian gestured dismissively at her wrap. "This old thing? I picked it up secondhand years ago for five bucks. I've no idea what it's made of—muskrat, beaver? I don't much care, because even in this polar vortex what all, it's incredibly warm."

"And it's incredibly uncool," Paige said.

"I guess *warm* and *uncool* mean kind of the same thing," Baba inserted gamely, and the girlfriend glowered.

It took Jillian a moment to register that she and Paige had managed a disagreement, a serious disagreement, with Jillian not two minutes in the door. "I bet the animals that gave up their lives for this coat were dead before I was born," she submitted. "Even if we leave aside the question of whether they'd have been bred and raised in the first place without a fur trade, my refusing to wear this coat doesn't bring the critters back to life, does it? I mean, why not redeem their sacrifice?"

"Because walking around in a barbaric garment like that is like voting," Paige countered. "It's advertising the killing of animals for the use of their body parts."

"Isn't that what we always do when we eat meat?" Jillian asked tentatively.

"I don't eat meat," Paige said stonily.

"Well, then, you're admirably consistent. Fortunately it's nice and warm in here," Jillian said, slipping off the *barbaric garment*, "so we can dispatch with the conversation piece." She braved a despairing glance at Baba, and she probably shouldn't have.

Once the threesome was settled in the living room—it might have been more graceful if Jillian had a date, too, but she hadn't been about to rent one—she was able to take the measure of Baba's new heartthrob. Late thirties; shorter than Jillian, but then most women were. After they did the whole where-are-you-from bit, it was clear that the girlfriend's Maryland accent had been thoroughly compromised by a northern education and academic colleagues from all over the map, leaving her vowels appealingly softened yet any suggestion of the hayseed picked clean. Paige had a compact figure and a somber, muted style: neat, close-cut hair, sweater, wool slacks, and now rather out-of-fashion Ugg boots. She was nice looking, though an incremental disproportion about her features made her face more interesting than plain old pretty. In any case, her expression was etched with an alertness, or with whatever elusive quality it was that wordlessly conveyed intelligence, which made mere prettiness seem beside the point. If her bearing was a shade wary and withholding, that could have been the result of circumstance. After all, a forgivable shyness and social discomfort could easily be mistaken for their more aggressive counterparts: aloofness and hostility. Jillian made a big effort thereafter to seem affable, expressing if anything excessive appreciation of the lentil salad and quinoa—but the whole rest of the evening was one long recovery from the fur coat.

In any event, that mild debacle was long behind them. By the time Paige graduated to Baba's Longest-Lasting Girlfriend Ever, Jillian made getting along with her a priority. There may have been an indefinable disconnect between the two women, but Jillian was sure they could bridge the void with the force of their good intentions. She wanted to have amicable relations with her best friend's girlfriend, and obviously Paige would want to have amicable relations with her boyfriend's best friend. Some inexorable transitive principle must have applied. If A likes B, and B likes C, then A likes C, right? And vice versa. Jillian wasn't a moron, either, and recognized the importance of taking a step back from Baba when Paige was present. Having known the woman's boyfriend for twenty-some years conferred an unfair advantage. Paige doubtless knew, too, that Jillian and Baba had slept together, and that was awkward.

Accordingly, Jillian came to pride herself on inserting an artificial distance between herself and her best friend during the numerous instances that she popped around for a drink or had the two of them over for dinner, sometimes further diluting the undiplomatic intensity between the two tennis partners by inviting another couple as well. In Paige's presence, she would ask Baba formal questions about the websites he was working on, when she was acquainted with them already, and had been discussing their particular annoyances après tennis for weeks. She was equally solicitous of Paige's travails in admissions, entering into the difficulty of balancing academic excellence with racial and economic diversity, or asking how you kept applicants from private schools from always having the edge—though this was the kind of stiff, topical discussion that Jillian didn't especially enjoy.

All told, she assessed her friend's transition to coupledom as a success for everyone concerned. Paige was on the serious side for Jillian's tastes, but as Baba pointed out, she had admirably strong convictions, of which Jillian had learned to be respectful (well—had learned to sidestep). Once Paige relaxed (which took at least a year), a sly, cutting sense of humor emerged—for example, in regard to college applicants who in their essays cast skiing holidays as "making a contribution to local communities." Jillian had come to appreciate Paige Myer, and she was grateful that finding a kindred spirit had so contented her best friend that he was considering coming off Zoloft. Jillian didn't quite understand what drew them together, but she didn't have to. She assumed that in private Paige shared her boyfriend's passion for parsing emotions and divining the fine points of complex relationships.

For that matter, Jillian largely failed to understand what drew anyone to anyone. It was one of those mysteries of the universe that the vast majority of people were able to convince someone else to singularly adore them, when any given suitor was free to choose from billions of alternatives—and these successful bondings encompassed portly shop assistants with prominent nose hair, severe-looking Seventh-Day Adventists with a penchant for hoarding felt-tip pens, and timid Filipina housemaids with wide, bland faces and one leg shorter than the other. It was astonishing that so many far-fetched candidates for undying devotion managed to marry, or something like it. Were it up to Jillian to fathom why her peers might logically invite lifelong ardor in order for them to pair off, the species would dwindle, until our worldwide population could snug into a boutique hotel. So what the hell, she'd long ago given up on second-guessing romantic attraction.

Meanwhile, Jillian had embarked on her most ambitiously futile project yet. Forty-three seemed just old enough to afford a retrospective. Were she a writer, she might have accrued sufficient experience to start a memoir. She was not a writer, but still being something of a curator of her own life, and having remained in the same cottage for fourteen years, she'd accumulated all manner of flotsam—the residue of multifarious adventures that she might convert from clutter to precious construction materials. At first she titled the assemblage "The Memory Palace," but the expression was derivative. At length, she settled on a fresher designation: "The Standing Chandelier."

A mbling into the living room in his bathrobe, Weston seemed to have walked into a conversation that, one-hand-clapping, was already under way.

"You know, this pretense Jillian has," Paige said, apropos of nothing, "that she's not really an artist—"

"Frisk likes to make stuff," he objected, rubbing his eyes. "That's all. It's posing as an Artist that's pretentious."

Paige was dusting. While any given day of the week was as good as any other to him, weekends meant something to her, and this swabbing, scouring, and polishing on a Saturday seemed a waste. The A-frame did have a more focused feel to it once she finished, even if he couldn't consciously detect how anything had changed. Yet the swish-swish of the cloth today conveyed an impatience. It may have been three in the afternoon, but he'd just gotten out of bed (having had to set his alarm to do so), and this was far too much vigor in his surround before coffee.

"But not really doing anything, and all her dumb little jobs. There's something a little spoiled about it."

"I don't follow," Weston said.

"It has to do with . . . class, really. Like, if she came from humble roots, having no ambition, and not participating in the art world proper, would seem like having low self-esteem. But because her father's a surgeon, being a big nobody is supposedly brave or something. Admirable and daring and original. Whereas the truth is that Jillian won't play the game because she doesn't want to lose." *Swish-swish,* went the cloth. "She's just afraid of judgment."

"Who wouldn't want to avoid *judgment*?"

"People who can make the grade, that's who. There's nothing upsetting about being judged if it turns out that everyone thinks you're wonderful."

"Uh-huh. And these days, when does that happen? Look at the internet. It's nothing but a lynch mob, braying about how shit everything is. I don't blame Frisk for not wanting to stick her neck out. Perfect formula for getting your head chopped off."

"She doesn't call herself an artist, because then she'd have to be a bad artist. Most of the junk she cobbles together is just—kooky. God, I wish you could find a way of telling her to stop bringing by those necklaces, made of feathers and, like, bat guano. You'd think she'd notice I never wear them."

This interchange required some serious caffeine, so Weston passed on the cafetière and went straight for the espresso machine. He was reminded that one thing he liked about Paige was pushback. When he and Frisk conferred, they tended to agree on everything, which was restful, but it wasn't sharpening. "*You* tell her to stop with the necklaces, then," he said.

"No, if I start telling Jillian what I really think, there's no telling where it will lead. Like, I can't bear the way she calls you 'Baba.' It's such a dumb name. Like rum baba, or baba ghanoush. Or like Bill Clinton's white trash nickname—*Bubba*."

"So is your problem that it's culinary, or that it's redneck?"

"My problem is it's not your name. And it's presumptuous. This little claiming, like, 'You're my special friend with a special name that I gave you that only I get to use.' You'd think she'd have the good grace to at least call you *Weston* when I'm around."

"It would sound artificial," he said wearily. "After well over twenty years? Like coming here and suddenly calling me 'Mister Babansky.'"

"I could live with 'Mister Babansky,'" Paige muttered. "A little regard for *boundaries* would be more than welcome."

Weston always woke slowly, emerging from bed in a bumbling, bearlike state that Paige commonly found beguiling; on more promising Saturday afternoons, she'd have tackled him back to the sheets. One of the perks of keeping such different schedules was that sex was a daytime activity, which had nothing to do with sleep. Paige was an inventive lover, with an appetite her low-key apparel and cropped, easy-maintenance haircut might seem to belie. He was well aware that Frisk found his relationship a measure perplexing—she was never good at keeping such thoughts to herself, even if she imagined she was being tactful; Frisk's version of discreet was everyone else's foot-in-mouth disease—and the often psychotropic frenzies with Paige, whose exquisitely subtle breasts drove him wild, were a big piece of the puzzle. A piece he tended to underplay with Frisk. Guys had been thin on the ground for her recently, and he didn't want to rub her nose in his good fortune.

"The truth is," Paige continued, having moved on to Windexing the wineglass rings on the coffee table, "it kind of grates when you call her 'Frisk,' too. Like you're football buddies in a locker room. That last-name thing, it's a gruff, shoulder-clapping palliness you usually get over after high school."

Weston wondered whether he could train himself to refer to Frisk as *Jillian* at home. The rechristening would take vigilance, but if it made a difference to Paige, the effort might pay off. On the other hand, such constant mental editing was a drain. He didn't think of his tennis partner as *Jillian*, and he was well aware that a first-name basis in this instance would amount to a demotion. He would be humoring Paige, too, and that wasn't a direction he wanted to go. A matter for private debate later. In the interim, he would try to stick to pronouns.

Taking a slug of espresso, he shot an anxious glance at the clock. "What's biting your butt today?"

"Oh, we'd talked about asking Gareth, Helen, and Bob over in a couple of weeks—our usual History Department crowd—and then I thought, right, great, you're no doubt expecting we'll ask Jillian, too."

"We don't always ask her." Jesus, this was exhausting.

"No, but the last time we didn't, you just *had* to tell her all about the evening with Vivian and Leo—"

"I couldn't resist telling her about that nightmare 'free-form berry tart.' How the cream cheese pastry kept springing leaks and we had to put it in the freezer—"

"You said you thought she felt hurt."

"That may have been my imagination. She doesn't expect to come over every time we *entertain*." He didn't think of himself as someone who *entertains*.

"But whenever we knock her off the guest list, you feel guilty."

"A little guilty," he said, having considered the question for a moment. "And a little relieved. I don't enjoy being caught in the middle."

"Then don't put yourself in the middle."

"*Finding* yourself in a position isn't the same as *putting* yourself there."

"Oh, no? Anyone with volition in a position he doesn't like can move somewhere else."

He didn't have time for this. He pulled the chilled thermos from the fridge, collected his cell, wallet, and keys, and put them by the door. "At least if we did ask her," Weston tossed off on the way to the bedroom to dress, "with Gareth-and-Helen, and Bob, it would be balanced."

"Bob doesn't balance anything, because Bob is gay," she called after him. "I wish Jillian would at least get another boyfriend."

"You couldn't bear the last one!" Weston called, pulling on his shorts.

"He was an idiot. Jillian has terrible taste in men."

Tennis shoes in hand, Weston came back out pushing his head through his T-shirt. "Thanks."

Paige looked up sharply, taking in the garb. "But you're not 'a man.' To her. Supposedly." Her demeanor had suddenly frozen over.

"I'm running late. This'll have to wait." Weston yanked his laces, and headed to the carton of balls in the corner to withdraw a new can.

"But it's Saturday."

"Frisk . . . she . . . got inexplicably caught up in

something she's working on yesterday, and lost track of the time. Not like her, but anyway, we rescheduled. May not get our two hours on a weekend, but one's better than nothing. See you around six or so. Seven at the latest." With a wisp of a kiss, Weston snatched his racket and fled. If they did play two hours, he would not be home till eight.

He hadn't wanted it to be true, and Weston was as capable of self-deceit as the next person, whatever his pretensions to self-knowledge. So it had taken him too long to pick up the pattern. On Mondays, Wednesdays, and Fridays, Paige got in a bad mood.

W eston knew this much about himself: he was prone to confuse thinking about something with doing something about it. So as far as he was concerned, in often turning his mind to Paige's exasperating and no-little-inconvenient antagonism toward Frisk, he was doing his job.

That Saturday afternoon they were freakishly able to play not two hours but three. Afterward, as Weston kept glancing at his watch in the dimming dusk, Frisk urged him to attend a private unveiling of her latest project, about which she'd been oddly secretive for months. But despite all Weston's industrious cogitating, it was more challenging than it once had been to arrange to stop by Frisk's cottage on his own.

He introduced the idea to Paige the following week with an ingratiating cynicism that made him dislike himself.

"I have no idea what it is," he said, paving the way for what he didn't wish to regard as "permission" to visit his best friend after hours. "I only know she's made a big deal out of it, and she's been working on it for a bizarrely long time. You can be sure it's a little crazy, per usual."

"Can't she just bring it along this weekend, now that she's virtually invited herself to dinner with the history crowd? She could wrap it up in *birch bark*."

"I got the impression it doesn't transport easily. And whatever it is, I'd think you'd be glad to get out of pretending to admire it."

Weston himself had tried to maintain a studious neutrality in relation to Frisk's creations. He took at face value her reluctance to participate in the professional art world, and one upside to her having carved out the right to "make stuff" outside the aegis of galleries—she did give things away, but she never sold anything—should have been release from assessment. Yet it was infernally difficult to suspend your critical faculties. In cosmopolitan culture—and the better educated in isolated college towns like Lexington held on to every signature of sophistication for dear life—the impulse to appraise was deeply ingrained: this knee-jerk need to no sooner see, hear, taste, or read a thing than to determine how "good" it was. The fashioning of an opinion was almost synonymous with apprehension of the item in question, so that you hardly had a chance to take something in before you got busy deciding what you thought of it—as if failure to come up with an instantaneous verdict made you remiss, or slackwitted. So Frisk's often whimsical contrivances had given him practice at detachment. Surely there was something to be said for simply looking, without immediately going to work on an estimation, as if you were expected to value the article at hand for insurance purposes.

He did appreciate Frisk's refusal to acknowledge the artificial boundary between fine art and craft, a line she crossed merrily back and forth all the time. And in one respect he didn't resist discernment: whatever she made, she made well. If his casual attendance at various galleries in Lexington and even DC was anything to go by, that made her the exception among most would-be artists, whose technical proficiency was often woeful.

Frisk was a better-than-competent carpenter and a skillful welder. The phantasmagoric tiling affixed to her claw-foot bathtub was neatly grouted. Her coffee table slatted together from logoed yardsticks, which hardware stores gave away to customers for free advertising in the 1970s, wasn't only ingenious, and nicely variegated with accents of red and yellow, but flat. Composing her pointillistic self-portrait made entirely of buttons, she had meticulously picked the residual threads from the holes of the secondhand ones, and had sacrificed several of her own shirts when the color of their fasteners helped fill out the demanding proportion of the surface taken up by the mass of hair—even if the resultant facial expression was unnervingly dazed. However wonky and unwearable Paige might find those strings of beads and found objects, the necklaces would never fall apart—much to his girlfriend's despair.

Moreover, whatever withering appraisals others might level at what she never even dignified as "her work," Frisk wasn't hurting anybody. Every time he entered the house of horrors of a major newspaper, Weston elevated sheer harmlessness to the pinnacle of achievement.

She wasn't asking for much, either: a smile, a handclap, or a good long stare. Such modest acknowledgment was the least he could supply her, and having showered after tennis on a Wednesday in May, he braved Paige's tight-lipped silence and promised to be back for dinner.

Frisk met him at the door in one of her floor-length getups. Once black and dotted with tiny red chrysanthemums, the dress had grayed and relaxed from multiple washings. The fabric looked soft—not that he was about to touch it. The near rag had doubtless been cadged from a church basement jumble sale, but especially with the hair it cast her as a Pre-Raphaelite Ophelia. She'd arranged the living room lighting so low it was almost dark. In the middle, resting on her hand-hooked shag rug, loomed an obscure object over six feet tall, poking here and there against the drape of its bedsheet.

"Don't look now, but your house is haunted," he said, kissing her cheek hello.

"And how," she said, insisting on uncorking a Sauvignon blanc before the viewing. She wasn't usually this dramatic about unveilings, which had never been so literal. Ordinarily, whatever she'd made would be propped in a corner, and she'd point.

"I call it 'The Standing Chandelier,' and if I'm honest with myself, this time I really want you to like it." She clinked her glass against his. "Ready? Close your eyes."

Weston played along. There was a rustle, then a click.

"Now."

If a "chandelier," it was upside down. The object was more of a standing candelabra, with multiple branches welded onto a central trunk in an irregular, botanical pattern. It glittered with dozens if not hundreds of tiny lights, most of them white, with a few incidental accents of yellow and blue. On examination, the lights illuminated a host of miniature assemblages, like individual installations on a minute scale. He knew her life in sufficient detail to infer the provenance of their constituent parts. Her wisdom teeth—pulled in her midtwenties. An admission ticket to the Stonewall Jackson House, where she used to work. The ebony trident-shaped mute would be a memento from that hot fling with a violinist during the fiddlers' convention. The lavender roll tied with a bow he recognized as the last grip she replaced on her trusty Dunlop 7Hundred, and there were other tennis references, too. One of the arms of the candelabra was neatly wound with a busted string; another enclosure included a rubber vibration dampener and a puff of chartreuse that could only have been shaved from their usual Wilsons (extra-duty felt for hard courts). She'd discovered that delicate curlew skull on a walk along the Maury River, the long tweezer of a beak still perfectly intact; it was one of her prize possessions. He spotted some keys, perhaps to old apartments, like the share with that O'Hagan shrew; a diminutive pewter cowbell, a souvenir from the solo Alpine hike through Switzerland on which she got lost for three days; a ribbon-wrapped coil of hair, a distinctive henna with the odd blond highlight, which could only have been snipped from her own head.

There were signatures of childhood: a small windup heli-copter (which still worked); an inch-high troll doll trailing pink hair, meant to fit on the end of a pencil; a red-and-gold kazoo and a plastic whistle. The pair of red salt and pepper shakers hailed from her very first airplane journey—museum pieces, from a domestic in-flight meal. One round, green cloth cameo was embroidered with a spool of thread, another with a tent—though the merit badges were few, because Frisk hadn't lasted long in the Girl Scouts. The 1981 Susan B. Anthony silver dollar was a present from her father on her graduation from sixth grade, the shining feminist symbolism dulled somewhat when the coin was pulled from circulation.

She'd even fabricated exquisitely reduced versions of earlier handiwork. The self-portrait was duplicated with minuscule beads instead of buttons (and at two inches square, the facial expression was more focused). She alluded to the yardstick coffee table by gluing together a dollhouse edition made of painted flat toothpicks, their enamel repeating the red and yellow accents of the life-size version. The claw-foot bathtub was now shrunken to a hollow half acorn, its tiling painstakingly approximated by individual squares of glitter. A woven rug, about the size of a commemorative stamp, echoed the colors of the very carpet on which the chandelier stood.

But this contraption wasn't a tree of junk; it wasn't like opening a jumbled drawer in a study whose owner never cleaned out her desk. Each collection of objects was a composition, often enclosed in inventive containers: a bright

Colman's mustard tin with windows cut out; a classy Movado watch box with its dimpled satin pillow, from Frisk's one splurge on jewelry that wasn't from Goodwill; a wide-mouthed, strikingly faceted jar that he recognized as having once held artichoke-heart paste, because he'd given it to her on her last birthday. Some of the boxes were made of tinted transparent plastic, while the cardboard ones were wallpapered inside, with velvet carpeting or miniaturized hardwood floors. Each still life was lit, and she'd been scrupulous about hiding the wires in the tubular branches. As ever, the workmanship was sound, and when he gave the trunk a gentle shake, nothing rattled or fell off. What's more, the lamp spoke to him. It conveyed a tenderness toward its creator's life that would invariably foster in the viewer a tenderness toward his own.

"Well?" Frisk prodded. "You haven't said anything."

For once Weston didn't have to concentrate on with-holding judgment. As Paige had observed, there was nothing to be feared from judgment when everyone would say that what you'd made was wonderful. So that's what he did. He said, "It's wonderful."

"You like it!"

"I love it. It reminds me a lot of Joseph Cornell."

Her face clouded. "Who's that?"

"Well, so much for William and Lee's art education. Paige

and I saw an exhibit of his work at the National Gallery. He put all these bits and pieces in little boxes, and hung them on the wall."

"So you're saying it's imitative?"

"You can't copy someone you've never heard of. And the comparison is a compliment. That retrospective was one of the only exhibits Paige has dragged me to that wasn't a waste of time. Cornell strikes a great balance between serious art and a childlike, kind of sandbox fucking around. And to my knowledge, he never made any 'standing chandelier,' either. You know, what's especially amazing," Weston noted, taking a couple of steps back, "is that it works on every level. Each little arrangement is perfect. But it also works as a whole. It's like a Christmas tree you can keep lit year round."

She was so excited that it broke his heart to turn down her spontaneous invitation to stay for dinner. Nonetheless, they finished the Sauvignon blanc.

Weston had been contemplating the matter for a while, and it was a rare rumination that he hadn't chosen to bounce off Frisk. Paige came across at first as a little unadorned and sexless, which is why it had taken him a while to notice her when he was working with the admissions office on the William and Lee website. But that was before you took her clothes off. She had a perfectly proportioned body that made so many other women seem like mere packaging. To his surprise, too, the heat between them hadn't cooled once the novelty wore off. To the contrary, the more familiar they became with each other, the more they relaxed and let fly. Maybe it was advantageous that she didn't advertise herself as a honeypot—disguise would keep other men's hands off her—and he liked the sensation between them of having a secret. He recognized something in her, too—a difficulty in figuring out just how to be with people. When he saw this awkwardness in someone else, he could see how attractive it was when you didn't like artifice, and would rather be genuinely uncomfortable than insincerely at ease. He'd come to treasure her faux pas, like that fracas over Frisk's fur coat. Blurting about the "barbaric garment" had hardly oiled the wheels that night, but she couldn't help but say what she was thinking. Which made it so much easier to trust her.

Paige was the more determined to overcome this inbuilt ungainliness, and her being more sociable than he was—the sociability was a discipline; her doses of company were almost medicinal—had so far been beneficial. Since they'd been together, he'd increased his circle of acquaintances by a factor of three, and now, haltingly, counted one or two as friends.

She took an interest in the arts, especially visual art. While many of the exhibitions they'd traveled to see had left him cold, there were memorable exceptions. After years of Frisk's jaundiced views of the museum and gallery establishment, he was grateful to be introduced to a few painters and sculptors who weren't phony. Paige conceived fierce opinions, while he was more wont to see multiple sides to an issue, so she pushed him profitably to stop waffling: yes, on balance, it did seem that the bulk of climate change was probably man-made. Few women would have been so tolerant of his late hours, too. (Some internal clock in him was six to seven hours out of sync with other people's. Try as he might, he could never hit the sack at midnight. Aiming for a more civilized schedule, he'd set an alarm for nine a.m., not arise until eleven, and still feel so cheated of sleep that the following day he'd snooze through the afternoon.) What's more, Paige accepted his mood swings. When he stopped talking and sank in front of late-night TV for days on end, she recognized the funk for what it was and didn't take it personally.

He'd worried at first about the vegetarianism, but they'd worked it out. At home, he'd eat legumes and eggplant, and the new dishes she brought to their table richly expanded his gastronomic range. He was "allowed," if that was the word, to order meat when eating out, so long as he brushed his teeth as soon as he got back.

He was forty-eight. He was pulling in a good living at last, and was surprised that making money made him feel more emotionally grounded; perhaps financial precariousness induced instabilities of other sorts. In the last thirty years, he had sampled enough women to have lost interest in variety. An isolate, he'd always thought of himself as a man who treasured his solitude above all else. Yet the last year and a half of cohabitation had been effortless, which wasn't so much a tribute to Lonely Guy Gets a Life as it was to Paige Myer in particular. He suffered under no illusion that he'd grown into a more accommodating character. The women he could put up with who could also put up with him were very few, if indeed there was more than one.

Leery of restaurant theatricality, Weston didn't feel the need to conspire with a chef to plant a ring in the molten middle of a flourless chocolate cake. Yet the day after the viewing of the chandelier, he did offer to make dinner (a zucchini lasagna with pecorino and béchamel), and he opened a red whose cost exceeded his usual $12 limit. It wasn't ideal to have chosen a weeknight, but he was eager to erase Paige's irritation that he'd stayed too long at Frisk's the previous evening, for which a motherfucking marriage proposal was sure to compensate. Eagerness outweighed anxiety. He was optimistic.

"But from your description," Paige said, digging into her lasagna, "it sounds goofy. Busy and trashy and kitchen sink."

The confounded thing was that Paige bent over backward to see the goodness in just about anybody else. She had a weakness for social strays, dragging home office assistants with bottle-bottom glasses and bad dandruff the way other women adopted mangy, big-eyed kitty cats with no collar. The only person in the world about whom he'd heard her be overtly unkind was Jillian Frisk.

"Then you'll have to take my word for it." He didn't want to get short-tempered, this of all nights. "I thought it was beautiful."

"Still." She wouldn't let it go. "You have to admit that the whole concept is on the egotistical side—"

"It's a celebration," he cut her off. "Of a life, and it could be anyone's life. Warmth toward your own past, and a sense of humor about your idiosyncrasies, doesn't make you self-obsessed."

He was overdoing the defense, but Weston was tired of being enticed into criticizing his best friend, which made him feel weak and two-faced. Yet somehow he had to imbue this meal with a more convivial vibe or put off his proposal for another time. For that matter, maybe what was making him testy was having an agenda and not addressing it. He and Paige were now sufficiently attuned that whenever one of them suppressed a thought, the atmosphere queered. So, with a deep breath, he refilled their glasses to announce,

"Look, I was going to wait until after dinner, but if I don't get this out I'm going to bust."

She immediately looked frightened—withdrawing from her food with a stricken wince, as if he'd just destroyed her appetite. If he weren't so determined to plow ahead, he might have considered that terrified reaction. He trusted her, but maybe the trust didn't run both ways.

He moved the plates out of the way, leaned in, and slid his glass forward until it kissed hers. "I shouldn't really be taking this hand," Weston extemporized, holding her fingers between his, "when I want to ask for it."

Either the construction was too clever, or fear had clouded her wit. She looked uncomprehending.

"I'm asking you," he spelled out, "to marry me."

"Oh!" Breaking the clasp, she sprang back, and her eyes filled with tears.

Now it was his turn not to get it. "Is that a yes?"

"I don't know."

This wasn't going the way he expected. The lasagna was starting to congeal.

"It's too soon? Too sudden? Too . . . what?"

Paige stared at her lap, worrying her napkin. "I want to be able to say yes. But I talked about this for a long time with my sister, more than once. I made her a promise, which was really a promise to myself. I can't tell you how hard it is for me to be disciplined about this. I'd love to throw my arms around you and say, 'What took you so long?' But I can't accept unconditionally."

"What's the condition?" A lump was already wadding in Weston's gut. He didn't bother to formulate to himself the nature of her stipulation, since she would spit it out soon enough. But he could have anticipated the ultimatum without much strain.

"Jillian," she said.

Lord, how lovely it would be, once in a while in this life, to be surprised.

"You know how you meet some people and think they're really great right away?" Paige continued. "But then they don't wear well, and what was superficially appealing is disappointing or even annoying in the long run. And then there are the other people, who you don't take a shine to at the start—who seem like creeps, or drive you nuts. But you stick with it, and get to know them better, and little by little they grow on you after all. So it can turn out that it's the very people who put you off at the beginning who you end up liking better than anybody."

Despite himself, Weston's expression must have looked hopeful.

"Well, this thing with me and Jillian isn't like either of those," Paige said, meeting his eyes at last, and that was that for feeling hopeful. "I couldn't stand her when I met her, and I can't stand her now that I've gotten to know her better. She acts as if her not doing anything professionally makes her so special, when most people don't do anything. She absolutely has to be the central focus in any given group of people, and whenever conversation strays from *her* latest goofball project, or *her* latest goofball outfit, she stops paying attention. She's basically undersocialized. She only pretends to be interested in anyone else—though I guess the pretending means she's socialized to a point—and whenever she asks about my life, it's obvious she's only going through the motions and doesn't care. I'm not even convinced she's that interested in you. You're just a great audience for her, and that's the main thing she needs from anybody. She has no sense of tact—which is just another form of being inconsiderate, of not bothering to pay attention to anyone else. So it never occurs to her to maybe keep her mouth shut about how great *fracking* is, because other people present might find her idiotic opinions offensive. For that matter, her opinions about anything important are all over the map. Since she doesn't read newspapers or even watch TV news, I've come to the conclusion that she doesn't *have* opinions—she just tries on a position like another outfit. She's not a serious person, West! She lives her life in, like—a playroom! And there's something so *crafted* about her. All presentation, no substance. With these big stagey entrances she makes. With all the feathers and jumped-up enthusiasm. It's fake. I have no idea what's behind the prima donna song and dance, aside from a woman who's hopelessly self-centered, and maybe a little lost. Like a lot of people who come across as egotistical, all that high-octane vivacity *could* be just overcompensating for underconfidence—since she's clearly too frightened to go out into the world and make her mark. That's me bending over backwards to be understanding, but I'm not a gymnast. I can't maintain that position for very long."

This—whatever you call the perfect opposite of *ode*—came out in such a rush that Paige was breathing hard. Weston asked dryly, "Is that all?"

"No, come to think of it. She also drinks too much. Way too much, making her a bad influence. Every time you go over there without me, you come back soused."

"Are you trying to convince me to despise my own best friend?"

"No, this is obviously my problem—but it's getting worse. Like those private coinages of hers that she repeats all the time whenever we go over for dinner, and she *always* serves popcorn as an appetizer? Which is cheap, by the way, in every sense. Practically free, and déclassé. So a substandard bowlful always has 'low loft.' Having only a few dead kernels at the bottom indicates a 'high pop ratio.' A batch lifting the lid on the pot is 'achieving lidosity.' You think it's enchanting, and I'm glad for you about that, I guess. But I couldn't find it enchanting on pain of death. I think it's dorky. Every time she says this stuff it's fingernail-on-a-blackboard for me. Her very *voice* grates. You'd think she'd learn to speak at a volume that isn't pitched for the hard of hearing! The stress of pretending to get along with her is wearing me out."

"If you want to keep the socializing to a minimum—"

"If it were just a matter of your friend getting on my nerves, maybe I could simply avoid her, and we could keep making excuses for why I'm busy and can't come with— though if we're really talking about getting married, a there's-somewhere-I-gotta-be routine could be hard to keep up over a lifetime. She'd figure it out. And then it would be an issue, and she'd get all touchy and wounded the way she does. Still, maybe that would be manageable. If that were the only problem, we could choreograph some sort of elaborate dance and never end up in the same room.

"But it's worse than that. She acts as if she owns you. I'm never sure what you two are talking about all that time after tennis—because you're always gone for way longer than the couple of hours you play. I can't help but worry that you're talking about me. And I worry the discussion isn't always nice, since nice things are usually a little boring, and for some reason they never take very long to say. I can't bear this paranoia. It's worse than when you go see your shrink. At least a shrink is supposed to keep his mouth shut, and be a little objective. If you also need to confide in a regular person, a civilian, and I'm going to be your wife, then you should be confiding in me."

"I can confide in more than one person, can't I?"

"You can confide in more than one person who's a *man*. You're going to claim I'm 'insecure.' Maybe I am, but maybe I have a right to be. If you two always had a platonic relationship, that would be one thing. But you've been involved with each other, you said, not once, but twice. You've played it down, but I've gotten the impression that both times it was kind of a big deal."

"We've both been involved with multiple people since. That's ancient history."

"It doesn't come across as ancient history. I still pick up a feeling between you two. It's not—well, it's not wholesome. There's an electricity, an energy, and it leaves me out. When she's around, you hardly touch me, have you noticed? Structurally, this situation is lopsided, too. I've had boyfriends, but then I've broken up with them or they with me, and we've gone our separate ways. I don't have anyone in my life who remotely duplicates Jillian's role in yours. I don't see anybody else socially three or four times a week, not even a girlfriend. I'd appreciate your trying to picture how you might feel if I saw one of my exes that often. And we hung out on a park bench for hours at a time and shared each other's secrets. Wouldn't that make you anxious? Wouldn't you worry what we talked about?"

"Half the time, it's about how many minutes you should sous vide salmon."

"Right—*half* the time. Wouldn't you worry about the other half? And imagine if this male pal of mine went through long periods of being unattached, and gave every sign of being emotionally dependent on me, to say the least. I think you'd get the jitters. Especially if this hypothetical guy was—I'll give Jillian this much, and I might feel a little different if she weren't—fucking good-looking." Paige didn't often curse.

Maybe this was where he was supposed to say, *Only up to a point*, or *But she's not aging very well*, or *I've never noticed one way or another*, or *Fair enough, but not my type*, further gilding the lily with the white lie, *I may not have mentioned it, but truth is we were a lousy match in the sack*. Maybe out of loyalty he was even supposed to claim, *Give me a break! Between the two of you, you're the knockout in my book*. There was no way any man in this position could remain in the realm of credibility and win.

"It's hardly her fault that most people would consider her reasonably attractive." Judicious. But even his insertion of *reasonably* was pure suck up, and probably backfired.

The qualifier made him sound evasive and condescending.

"The issue isn't 'most people.'"

"I don't think of her that way."

"So you've told me repeatedly. Whatever folks say over and over starts sounding shifty. As if they're trying to talk themselves into something."

"I don't know what else I can say to make you feel safe."

"There's nothing you can say. That's the point. There's something you'd have to do."

Weston wished that real life had a pause button. When watching a smart TV, you could always freeze the frame before an exciting scene, and leave to take a leak or grab a snack. Meantime on-screen, no one pushed the protagonist off a ledge to fall twenty stories to the pavement. As if to activate his personal remote control, he found himself sitting perfectly still. If no one spoke, and no one moved, he and Paige could remain in this instant and not the next one. As soon as the program advanced, they would be living in a different world where his life was bound to be worse. For when you said things, there was no taking them back. That was the other button real life lacked: a rewind.

Paige said, "You have to stop seeing her."

"That's out of the question." The answer was reflex.

She started to cry. Weston realized they'd been talking several feet apart, and any man who did not rise and comfort his lover when she was weeping was a monster. He was not a monster.

"That was what I told my sister you would say." She snuffled on his shoulder and got a string of watery snot on his shirt. "And it's okay. It's all my fault, in a way. This isn't the first time I've fallen in love with the wrong man. I just didn't—read the situation right. I took you at your word that you were free, but you're not free. Because all this time I think you've been in love with Jillian. With *Frisk*. She probably loves you, too, and I don't know why you two aren't together already. It seems like a bad-timing problem, but I wish you'd figure it out, or you'll just put your next girlfriend through the same thing. I wish I'd understood what was going on sooner, because for me it's too late. Now I'm going to feel horrible. I'd have loved to marry you. I thought that after so many dead ends I'd finally found someone. But it's like Princess Diana said: 'There have always been three people in this relationship.' I can't marry you if it means constantly having to look over my shoulder. Wondering where you are and what you're saying about me and why it's taking you so long to come back from the tennis court."

They had sex that night, but in a spirit of Paige's sacrificing herself on the altar of him. She was too wide open, defenseless, almost splayed. The feel was a little warped. As they coupled, too, he couldn't help but notice the odd tear drizzle down her temple and pool in her ear. He was so afraid that she was thinking this was the last time that he couldn't ask. When her alarm went off, though neither was rested, he got up with her, as if now she were the one who shouldn't be trusted, and had to be watched.

Before she left for work—where she would be useless, and coworkers would ask if something was the matter; her face was puffy and bruised looking, her eyes squeezed and red— he sat her down. Listen, he said. What she was asking was monumental. He and Frisk had been fast friends for—Yes, yes, Paige interrupted wearily. *Twenty-five years.* He wasn't refusing to comply with her wishes outright, he said. But he wasn't an impulsive man, and it took him longer than most people to know his own mind. So she had to let him consider this. In the meantime, he said, he had to know what he was considering. The details. She wasn't saying that he had to see Frisk less often, or with a chaperone, but that he had to cut off the friendship altogether? Paige nodded. And that included tennis? When he asked for that last clarification, it was hard to get the words out. In some ways, she said, especially tennis. Okay, he said, so what was the time frame? (He worried he was sounding too businesslike, but there was clearly an element here of drawing up a contract.) For the first time since she imploded the night before, Paige looked a measure less crestfallen—no, a measure less *destroyed*. She had never looked *crestfallen*, but *destroyed*. The time frame? she repeated. In the instance that he'd really do as she asked? So that they were getting married after all? Well, she had obviously put up with this situation as his girlfriend, she said, and for longer than she should have. But she wasn't putting up with it as his wife. Assuming they weren't talking about some old-fashioned long engagement, he would have until their wedding day to sort it out. To say good-bye, and give Jillian his good wishes, or whatever it was that people did when they'd never speak to each other again.

"This is a small town," he reminded her. "We'll run into each other regardless."

"Okay, I'm not being ridiculous," Paige said, rolling her eyes. "You can still say hi. But you might find in the end you'd be doing her a favor. I mean, why *is* a woman that good-looking still single in her midforties? She may not realize it, but she could be holding out for you. In any case, she certainly uses you as a crutch. If you let her go, she might find someone. As things stand, she doesn't feel the need to do online dating or anything. She always has her *Baba*, like a stuffed bear."

There was a final condition. About the wedding, if there was one—here and only here did Paige sound a note of vengefulness—"*She's not invited.*"

When he reran that conversation with Paige after she left for the university, Weston was alarmed by how rapidly their tenses had changed, from the conditional/subjunctive to the simple future to the present. "You *would* have until the wedding" had slid to "We *will* run into each other," until Paige was allowing, "You *can* still say hi." Although officially no decision had been taken, the very grammar of this dilemma was moving too fast and getting away from him.

It would have to be a tennis day. Having clocked the day of the week, Paige had charged at the door, "You're going to tell her, aren't you? About the whole conversation, and my awful ultimatum, and then you'll decide what to do about it *together*."

The nasty twist of that parting shot, which he left unanswered, alone illustrated how impossible this situation had grown overnight. Preserving his nonaligned status by being so stoically methodical with Paige before she left, he had tried to carve out extra time for himself, in which to examine all the angles. Yet absent resolution, staying in the same house with Paige even one more day could prove untenable. The longer he delayed giving his girlfriend an answer, too, the more he'd express being torn—the more he'd indicate that marriage to Paige wasn't important enough for him to pay a price for it, and the more he'd indicate that his friendship with Frisk was *too* important. Weston's mind was forever chewing mental cud, and he wasn't accustomed to having to do something rather than merely mull it over. Starkly, either he announced this very evening that a detonator was ticking on his friendship with Frisk, or Paige moved out.

Over a sodden bowl of muesli, fragments of that excoriation of Frisk kept hitting his brain like shrapnel. He supposed that, looked at a certain way, some of his girlfriend's accusations were sort of true. Frisk was a little self- . . . self-centered, self-involved, self-absorbed? But who wasn't self-something? It might not have been obvious from the outside, but he himself was wholly and unapologetically self-absorbed. His own nature may have been the source of endless frustration, but of tireless fascination also, to the point where he regarded the study of Weston Babansky as his real career.

Besides, he wondered if you couldn't describe just about anyone in terms that were both accurate and lacerating. You could probably savage the personality of everyone on the planet if you wanted to, though there remained the question of why you would want to. And some folks were destined to stand more in the firing line than others. Frisk had a flamboyance that thrust her head above the parapet. She was something of an acquired taste, but Weston had acquired it, and he worried that Paige's aspersions might make him more critical, more susceptible to perceiving what had so recently seemed his best friend's strengths as her flaws. After all, any virtue could be cast as a defect. Optimism might look like credulity; self-assurance could come across as conceit. So while he clearly shouldn't repeat any of Paige's broadside to Frisk, he'd also have to be mindful about not rehearsing the diatribe in his own head. The recollection made him shudder. It was called "character assassination" for good reason. He felt as if he'd witnessed a murder.

Exhausted, he'd be sluggish on the court. How extraordinary, that he wasn't looking forward to a hit.

Mobilizing his gear that afternoon as if sloshing through floodwater, Weston acknowledged that the one thing he did owe his girlfriend was some serious soul searching. Maybe there was something wrong with his relationship with Frisk, something unsavory. Maybe they crossed a line. Truly, Paige didn't demand the same broad-mindedness from him. He had difficulty conjuring a mirror image in which Paige ran off to spend hour upon hour with another man, of whose intentions he was suspicious. The imaginary rival remained a paper doll. Yet she had to be right. He wouldn't like it.

Presumably when meeting as veritable strangers on the street they would learn to say hi, but they didn't bother with formal greetings yet. Leaning against her bike, helmet off and headband on, Frisk simply raised her eyebrows and laid a censorious finger on her watch. He was fifteen minutes late.

Silent chiding sufficed, and she let the annoyance go. "You know, I've been flying on such a high ever since you came to see the chandelier," she jabbered en route to the net post. "I'm so excited you like it!"

He wanted to ask, *Do you worry that my reaction to your lamp thing, or anything else really, matters too much to you?* But he didn't.

"You're quiet," she noted, unsheathing the Dunlop 7Hundred.

"I didn't get much sleep."

"You're not getting down in the dumps again, are you?"

"You could say that," he conceded.

Frisk's magenta shorts were on the skimpy side, and as he watched her sashay to her baseline Weston concluded that she wasn't wearing underwear. She should be wearing underwear, shouldn't she? Something sporty with wide elastic—a little baggy, cotton, and plain.

*Was he still attracted to her?* Well, what did that mean? That he wanted to jump her? That he actively thought about fucking her? No, he didn't. He didn't think he did. He had, after all, fucked her already, which strangely enough, though he was not a linguistic prude, he didn't like the sound of. He could naturally recall those two periods when they got down to it—perhaps the affairs were only a few months apiece, though in his head they took up the space of a few years. The memories were stored more as a jagged sequence of stills than as video. In the rare instance that these images strobed his mind, he tended to flinch. He no sooner summoned what she looked like naked than made the picture go away.

"Baba, I know you're tired," she shouted across the net. "But I don't usually start a point and you just stand there!"

"Sorry," he called from his baseline. "Distracted."

She was a comely woman and he was a hale heterosexual whose testosterone levels had not yet dropped to zero. She had good legs—long and sinewy, with well-developed calf muscles, though in her forties the skin above her knees was starting to crinkle, from years of too much sun. She had a taut figure, and hilarious hair. He loved her face, though he didn't know what that meant, either, except that it was true: he loved her face. Blue eyes with shocks of green, thin lips and a mouth slightly too wide, and he liked it wide. Yet this breakdown was unhelpful. He treasured her *presence*. He was accustomed to her *presence*, at ease in her *presence*, and her appearance was utterly inseparable from the whole of her: the whooping laugh, the zany ideas, the unreliable crosscourt backhand. So the answer to his point of inquiry was a worthless *I don't know.*

Weston did at last bear down on the ball, focus on which reprieved him from still more mental cud chewing that resolved nothing. They were well matched in a broad sense, but who was beating whom swung drastically back and forth from session to session and hour to hour, and by the end he was getting the better of her. In fact, during the final thirty minutes he marshaled a degree of sheer power from which he may often have sheltered her, perhaps subconsciously. She could hit a heavy ball for a woman, but he still had the gender advantage if he chose to employ it.

"You know, you seemed almost angry," she said on the bench. "I'm used to your getting mad at yourself, but toward the end there you seemed mad at me."

The distance between their thighs was about an inch. Which wasn't enough if she didn't have any panties on, and Weston discreetly rearranged himself farther away.

"I'm not angry at you. I was just trying to really connect for once."

He was dismayed that she accepted the denial so readily —"You sure wore me out, anyway!"—before segueing to her current fixation without dropping a beat: "By the way, you were right about that Christmas tree quality. I've started leaving the chandelier on at night while turning all the other lights off, and it's magical. Every December when I was little, I used to get up at six a.m. even when school was out—so I could listen to "Pavane for a Dead Princess" turned down low and bask in the glow of the tree. I was always crushed whenever my parents finally decided it was too dried out and a fire hazard. Now I don't ever have to take down the tree."

She was irritating him, and it was a terrible feeling. Maybe Paige was right, that this chandelier contraption was egomaniacal. And he'd never noticed before how often his tennis partner touched his arm while she talked.

Frisk went on to explain about how she'd started making her own kimchi and the smell was taking over the whole cottage. He shared a recipe he'd tried recently, a new twist on crab cakes, but his heart was so little in the telling that he forgot to mention the mango chutney—and that was the twist.

Weston's subsequent non sequitur was not premeditated. Nevertheless, he needed to investigate the question pressing in on him: *Is there something wrong here, have we all along been doing something wrong?* So after she related how last week during a tutorial her student kept emitting such evil farts ("there must be an intermediate state in physics that's halfway between a gas and a solid") that she had to keep excusing herself for a bathroom break or drink of water just to get out of the room, he said, "Oh, right. I asked Paige to marry me last night."

Dropping that bombshell was an observational experiment. He watched her face. The face that he loved—that he either loved innocuously or loved dishonestly. Whatever was happening in that face, it was complicated. Which meant something in itself. And her pause implied a reckoning. Did one *reckon* with good news?

"Wow," she said after the elongated beat. "You've sat here all this time, telling me a slightly lame recipe for crab cakes, and then it's like, also, I'm getting married, and don't forget the cilantro?"

"We've never been hung up on telling stories in hierarchical order."

"If an extraterrestrial spaceship had landed on the Chevaliers' lawn this morning, I think I might have let you know before telling the anecdote about Fart Boy."

*Equates Paige with invader from outer space.*

". . . was this proposal something you've been planning for a long time?"

*From very outset, solely concerned with whether Baba has been concealing his intentions from her.*

"A while."

"I'm surprised you've never mentioned the idea. Mister Mysterious!"

*Inference corroborated. Subject cares more about enjoying privileged communication with ostensible "best friend" than about life-changing content of revelation. Indicative of narcissism and/or unhealthy obsession with Baba–Frisk relationship.*

"I don't tell you everything," he said.

"Oh, you do, too!" she exclaimed, prodding his arm again.

"I don't even tell myself everything."

"You tell me what you haven't told yourself. That's one of the main things I'm for."

"I do occasionally talk to my own girlfriend," he reminded her.

"All lovers require editing. That's why I can tell you that 'I'm so aroused!' is a turnoff, but I wouldn't have told Sullivan that in a million years."

*Implicitly relegates Baba–Paige relationship to subsidiary status. Marriage proposal = emotional trump, palpable evidence that Baba–Paige relationship is primary. Subject in denial.*

"You know, you still haven't asked if Paige said yes," he said.

"Well, of course she did. She's smitten with you. It's amazing you didn't call to cancel tennis, because she'd already dragged you off to the registrar at town hall."

*Instinctively associates Baba getting married with not playing tennis. Good guess, by coincidence, but for Frisk, not playing tennis = end of world [see ET mention above; Paige = calamity/Armageddon]. Once again, Paige/marriage = threat.*

On reflection, since he had plenty of experience with therapy, Weston added a second note: *Describes Baba–Paige relationship in terms suggesting unequal emotional involvement. More comfortable with Paige being "smitten" w/ Baba than w/ Baba being smitten with Paige. Assumes Paige must be driving force behind marriage ("dragged" to town hall), imputing passivity or unwillingness to Baba.*

"You don't seem all that happy about my news," he submitted carefully, as if dropping a catalyst into a test tube with a pipette.

"I might be happier if you seemed happier. But you're acting so morose. I asked before we played if you felt down, and you said yes. That's not the way I'd expect you to feel after popping the question. Hey"—another touch, on the shoulder—"maybe not leaping and frolicking, but at least a smile?"

*Actively looks for signs that Baba does not really want to marry Paige.*

His obligatory smile was pained.

"Are you sure this is a good idea?" she pressed on.

*Actively dissuades Baba from marrying Paige.*

"When am I ever sure of anything?" he said. "Except that obviously, if I did propose, then on balance I decided that yes, it's a 'good idea.'"

"Then why are you so disturbed?"

*Deliberately exaggerates what Baba believes is carefully controlled affect.* But Weston could no longer sustain a clinician's arch distance, and put down his mental pen.

*Why am I disturbed?* he considered. *Let me count the ways. Because I am starting to see things from my lover's point of view, and I don't want to. Because from that perspective, I am either a cruel two-timer or conveniently delusional. It seems that I have been trying to have it both ways at a good woman's expense. I put my would-be fiancée through unnecessary suffering out of selfishness. I have heard my whole life that men and women can never be friends. I have nursed the vain notion that you and I are exceptions to that rule, not because this is necessarily true, but because being a supposed exception suits my purposes: I can have my cake and play tennis with it, too. But I am also disturbed because I love you, and whether that love is corrupt, or covertly flirtatious, or interfering with my ability to fully embrace another woman without holding something back, it is still love, in all its near-indestructible dreadfulness, and I am about to take a sledgehammer to my own heart.*

"Oh," Weston said lightly. "You know me, I'm moody."

Jillian inevitably contemplated the matter, and would have liked to have been happier, which wasn't the same as being happy. But then, while many people are overjoyed when they decide to get married themselves, it's hardly normal practice to hoot and sing hallelujah when someone else does. Understandably, too, Baba's new circumstances underscored her own—she hadn't even dated for over a year—and thus his announcement moved her to feel a tad pensive, a degree more concerned that she for one was destined to remain single. Worse things could happen, of course. Having proved in Jillian's experience more durable than romance, friendship often provided a form of companionship as good as marriage, if not better.

When she scrutinized herself—which made her feel like Baba—she didn't appear to feel doleful or pissed off or excluded, because she was already integrated into Paige and Baba's social life. Paige was already acclimated to her boyfriend's amity with an old college classmate, which had lasted his adulthood through. So there was no reason that anything would change after a wedding. Apart from a possible honeymoon, it would be back to tennis and a musing debrief thrice a week, punctuated by twosome, threesome, and several-some dinners, liberally lubricated with libation.

Any self-interested consternation that Baba was taking himself off the market would be irrational. Back in the day, they had each had opportunity to pursue the other as marriageable material, and they had each walked away. The two of them as an item were not meant to be. What was meant to be was exactly what they were. In fact, in the more recent go-round, Jillian had been the one who'd cut it off, and she could never bear women who got huffy when other women picked up their discards. You either wanted a guy or you didn't. If you didn't, it made no more sense to get retroactively possessive than it did to become incensed that a neighbor was walking around in a shirt that you'd donated to the Salvation Army.

Yet the following several weeks felt indefinably out of kilter. If this summer were a bed, it would be rumpled and unmade. Baba canceled tennis dates more often than he once did (that is, he canceled at all). Shit happens, and she'd overlooked his being late that afternoon in May when he delivered the perplexingly leaden report of his proposal. But the tardiness grew chronic. She'd wait around for twenty minutes, fidgeting in anxiety that they'd lose no. 3—their favorite, if only for being customary—because a lone player couldn't hold a court. By the time Baba finally showed up, Jillian would have grown cross, which meant playing in a humor at odds with the buoyant spirit of the whole endeavor.

This was the summer, too, that she developed an odd glitch in her forehand follow-through—a destructive crook of the wrist as the ball left the strings that hooked the shot to the net. One of the commonalities that suited them to each other on court was a tendency to exasperation with the shortcomings of their own games and an inexhaustible patience in relation to the other's frustrations. So Jillian would have expected to grow provoked by the spastic innovation herself, but not for Baba to find it just as infuriating.

"You should really consider taking a few lessons," he announced testily on a water break. "Iron it out."

She was nonplussed. "Since when do we take lessons?"

"A little humility goes a long way in this sport, and a few sessions with a professional can be invaluable. I'm sure you could find a coach at William and Lee who moonlights. And it's not that expensive. If you don't think you can afford it, you can always go back to leading those tourist walkabouts around Lexington landmarks."

He knew full well she'd given up that part-time job because they weren't accommodating about releasing her on Monday, Wednesday, and Friday afternoons.

"But I know what I'm doing wrong," she said. "I just can't seem to stop."

"When I know I'm doing something wrong," he said tightly, "I stop."

Most disconcerting was Baba's new reluctance to linger after a session. There was always an appointment, or he'd promised to have an early dinner with Paige. Was he trying to establish some new protocol now that he was getting hitched? Meanwhile, Jillian had issued a routine dinner invitation to the couple—she reminded Baba that his fiancée had still not seen the Standing Chandelier, about which so far other friends had been spectacularly enthusiastic—but those two could never arrive at a date. She knew he'd come to cast a wider social net with Paige—all to the good, since in times past, tennis aside, unless Jillian hauled him through the door, he was capable of spending weeks on end holed up with a computer—but she hadn't thought he'd become one of those gadflies out and about every night. Hard to arrange anyway, in a town of eight thousand people.

She'd have understood his being busy and distracted if he and Paige were in the process of planning a massive wedding. But the event on August twenty-sixth was meant to be modest. The invitations apparently went out by email to a guest list of under fifty (Jillian was surprised they could even marshal these dozens of well-wishers when Baba had long been such a hermit, but then everyone had cousins). They were eschewing the catered cakes, goodie bags, and hired DJs of the marriage-industrial complex for a simple ceremony followed by a potluck picnic. That night, to make the day more of an occasion for out-of-towners, they'd have a party with drinks and snacks back at the A-frame, with music streamed from Baba's Mac. About all that would have been taking up her tennis partner's time was putting together the playlist.

Jillian had offered to ask the Chevaliers if they'd be open to letting the picnic take place on their grounds. In August, the estate's owners would be down in Byron Bay, Australia, and she was sure that they'd happily grant permission so long as everyone cleaned up after. The hills were rolling, the lawn luscious. It would be so much more private than the Boxerwood Nature Center, and not as impersonal as the Golf and Country Club, which would charge an arm and a leg—

"Jordan's Point Park," he cut her off. "It's pretty, it's public, and it doesn't involve easily offended rich people. But thanks anyway."

He didn't sound very thankful. "Okay, never mind, then."

By the fourth week of July, Jillian's follow-through glitch was worse than ever, losing her every third point or so. Constant apologizing made her meek, and meekness weakened her strokes, when one of the aspects of her game that Baba had always relished was that she gave as good as she got. She was playing like a girl. She was playing like a girl who sucked. Tennis was a hard enough sport without the additional burden of worrying that your partner was bored or otherwise not having a good time. And he was not having a good time—or at least that's what it looked like from the other side of the net that Friday, when he started losing numerous points from his own unforced errors, his motions phlegmatic, as if he couldn't be bothered to chase her dreary little shots. Careful not to seem pouty or petulant or weepy and instead making a matter-of-fact and indisputable observation that this wasn't working, Jillian suggested as they gathered balls at the net that they call it quits prematurely. It was the first time in twenty-five years that they'd curtailed their play in the absence of rain, dark, injury, or hail.

With the half hour's early retirement, for once Baba couldn't claim that he had to rush off elsewhere.

"Sorry," she said again on the bench. Though it must have been ninety degrees, so frequently had she futzed up that she'd barely worked up a sweat. "Maybe I should take those lessons."

"Yeah, maybe," he said, staring glassily straight ahead. He didn't seem very attached to the advice anymore.

When neither said anything for a couple of minutes, there was none of the serenity that usually characterized their silence. It was awkward. Awkward the way it would have been with just anyone.

"Baba." She took a breath. "Is there some reason that you and Paige can never find a single free evening to come to the cottage for dinner?"

"We have been pretty busy. But," he added, "it's possible I feel protective."

"How's that?"

Kneading his knees, he seemed to struggle with and overcome some impulse, and then to proceed in a spirit of grim resolution. "Well, face it, Frisk. As for the whole getting-married thing, you haven't exactly been on board."

"How can you say that? I think it's great! I think Paige is great! I think you make a great couple! One of those—unpredictable couples. Who might not be spit out as checking all the boxes on Match dot com, but who make a more interesting combination as a consequence of being unlikely."

"Is that a tortured way of telling me that you think Paige and I are a bad fit?"

"No, that's not what I meant, and not what I said, either. What's with you? I swear, all summer you've been so out of sorts! Constantly taking things the wrong way. Being grumpy and distant. Ever since—"

"That's right, *ever since*. Is this another plea to get me to call off the wedding?"

"When have I ever—"

"When have you not? It was obvious when I first told you we were getting married that you opposed the idea, and were hoping to talk me out of it. I don't know what your problem is with Paige—"

"I don't have a problem with Paige." He wouldn't look at her, so she leaned into his lap until he met her gaze. "I don't. I like her. We have a few negligible differences of opinion. I don't mind wearing a beat-up, used fur coat to keep warm. I could never give up veal chops. I'm of two minds about fracking because Virginia needs the money and I like the idea of energy independence, but that argument was stupid because I don't actually care that much one way or the other. What's important is she's honest, and sincere, and genuine, and forthright. She's nice-looking, she's obviously loyal, and she must be pretty smart if she went to Middlebury, though I like the fact she doesn't show off how much she knows. She's got a way bigger social conscience than I do."

Somehow the more Jillian piled on the compliments, the hollower they sounded, which drove her to pile on still more. "There's something disarming about her—something vulnerable and unguarded, so I guess I understand your impulse to 'protect' her, but she doesn't need protection from me. Why should she, when she's been nothing but nice to me, to a point where I've almost been embarrassed—

giving me that fringed shawl she found in Lynchburg, or the fig preserves from the Wine and Music Festival? Never mind if a present isn't all that expensive, it's the gesture. Thinking of me, even when I'm not there, and making a good guess as to what I might like. She's never seemed wary or territorial, despite the fact that you and I are so close. Which is pretty amazing, actually."

Throughout this panegyric touting the many fine qualities of his wife-to-be, Baba looked only the more miserable.

"Or we used to be close," Jillian added, sitting back.

"See?" Baba pounced. "That's what I mean. That kind of cutting aside, which says it all."

"Oh, all *what*? I'm very, very glad you've found someone. I don't know how to spell it out more plainly. Because what I appreciate most about Paige is that she loves you. It's obvious every time she looks at you. In fact, there are times she can't even bear to look at you, because it's too much, it makes her feel too much. Why wouldn't I want that for you?"

"That's what I ask myself," Baba said.

"I'm sorry if I didn't burst into tears of joy, or whatever you hoped for when you told me. You seemed in a terrible frame of mind, like someone had died or something, and I was trying to understand why, not 'talk you out of' getting married."

Yet the further she extolled his fiancée's merits, the more Jillian was reminded of that feeling in the presence of a woman who detested her: that no matter what she said, she was digging her own grave.

O nce back home, Jillian showered and put her feet up with a glass of wine in the glow of the chandelier. She considered whether the problem wasn't talk itself, with its deserved reputation as cheap. She could blah-blah herself blue in the face, and Baba would never be sure that she wasn't merely mouthing what he wanted to hear. That very afternoon, hadn't Jillian sung the praises of the gesture, which spoke so much more forcefully than words? Perhaps in this case a gesture of larger proportions than a jar of fig preserves.

When the ideal course of action presented itself, she felt a twinge, like a stitch in the side—which is how she could tell it was right. A grand gesture should cost you. The agonizing back and forth on a second glass of Chablis was self-theater. She had already made up her mind, and by the third glass had moved from fraudulent indecision to the early stages of mourning. Baba would believe that she was thrilled he was marrying Paige Myer only when he saw how much she was willing to surrender to make the point.

Packaging up that weekend was anxiety provoking, and required half a roll of six-foot Bubble Wrap and a full roll of packing tape. When tennis was rained out that Monday, Jillian was relieved; neither her game nor her friendship with Baba was going to settle until her alleged antagonism toward his impending nuptials was conclusively demonstrated to be all in his head. Though she didn't want him to feel ashamed of himself. She wanted him to be touched. Cancel that; she wanted them both to be touched.

On Tuesday, the weather cleared. After the Chevaliers' gardener, Lance, had finished for the day, he generously agreed to provide the services of his van. So extravagantly had Jillian wrapped her offering that, even with both of them manipulating the monster wad of pillowy plastic, it barely fit through the back doors. Lance drove, while she stayed in back to ensure their cargo didn't rock, and he was equally sweet about helping her unload. "I didn't go to this much trouble for me and my wife's twenty-fifth!" he said, pulling on the bundle's back end. "That sixty-inch Sony flat screen was a box of safety matches in comparison. Whoever these folks are, sweetie, you sure must like 'em."

"Yeah, that's the message, all right," Jillian said. It wasn't all that heavy with the two of them, but it was unwieldy, and got stuck again as she shoved it from behind. "Careful!"

she cried. "Don't put any pressure on it. Let's just *ease* it back and forth."

She hadn't given Baba a heads-up about her visit, lest he be driven to "protect" his fiancée from her fearsome disapproval. Besides which, you didn't give fair warning about a surprise; that was what made it a surprise. It was barely seven thirty p.m., still light, and Baba's Escort was in the drive.

"Where you wanna carry this, missy?" Lance asked, once the bundle had cleared the van's doors.

Dismally, Jillian appraised the A-frame's entrance. If her delivery jammed between the roof and floor of the van, it wasn't going to fit through the front door. "I'm afraid that to get it inside, I'll have to unwind the outside layers. If you keep it steady upright, I'll start slicing tape. Fortunately, I brought an X-Acto knife."

This was poor dramatics. She had hoped to make the present look less like a lifetime supply of plastic wrap by belting it with the red ribbon tucked in her shorts pocket. But it was too late for the flourish, because their commotion had already drawn Baba to the door.

In the middle of his front lawn, she was in the midst of walking another layer off the wad, which with all the packaging stood eight feet tall. To keep from having to feed the accumulating Bubble Wrap between Lance and the bale, she'd sliced off a couple of sections, now fluffing in the breeze and trashing up the yard. As Baba emerged onto the porch, she had to chase after one of the rectangles to keep it from blowing away.

"What's this about?" he asked, with an expression she couldn't read. If he knew what the object was, he gave no indication, but he might readily have guessed had he applied himself.

She smiled shyly, arms full of plastic. "It's your wedding present. I think I can get it through the door now. Want to help?"

The two men helped negotiate the slimmer but more fragile bundle, while Jillian, who was familiar with which bumps were the most delicate, directed its orientation. Once in the living room, she had them rest it on one side so that she could go at the bottom with the X-Acto knife, cutting away the packaging until she revealed the metal base. She'd been so busy with the logistics that it was only then that she looked up to meet Baba's gaze, though he had to have surmised some time before what they were unwrapping. His smile was warm enough, but also colored by a wan quality.

"Are you sure you want to give this away?" he asked quietly.

"To just anybody, no. To you—to you and Paige—sure as shootin'."

"But that thing took you six months."

"Longer. But if it didn't mean anything to me, it wouldn't be a good present."

They raised the new addition to Weston Babansky's already eclectic decor to its upright position, and with the base unpacked it was stable. Jillian assured Lance that she could take it from here, thanked him effusively, and wished him good-night. Yet it was several more minutes before Paige finally emerged from downstairs, carrying a basket of clean laundry. Had Jillian heard visitors muffling overhead, while the scraping of an obscure object penetrated the ceiling of her utility room, curiosity would have gotten the better of her sooner. Some women had a vigilant relationship to a load in the drier.

"Jillian!" Paige's face quivered briefly, as if she were about to sneeze. "What on earth? Is this that—chandelier thing?"

"I was thinking"—Jillian had unwound the big sheet now, and was down to snipping the smaller squares cushioning each individual assemblage—"that during the party on the night of the wedding, it would be nice to have a centerpiece. Which also provides romantic, indirect lighting."

"So this is a loaner?" Most people were a little graceless or flustered when on the receiving end of extreme generosity, and she wouldn't have meant to sound so hopeful.

"No, no," Jillian corrected. "That would make for a pretty

feeble wedding present. It's yours, and the welds are solid. As your grandchildren will discover, should you choose to go that direction."

Insofar as Jillian had envisioned this presentation, she'd imagined a bit more hubbub, especially since Paige had never seen the "chandelier thing" before. But the betrothed couple was unnervingly muted, so that when Paige offered a cup of tea, Jillian said maybe a glass of wine instead, if a bottle was open. A steadier. The trouble was, the unveiling was too fiddly and protracted, what with unwinding the individual strips of Bubble Wrap first from the miniature toy box and then from the helicopter inside, unpacking the cotton balls from around the curlew skull, checking that the wisdom teeth were still securely glued in place, and peeling off every little scrap of residual tape from the structure. On reflection, the theater would have been flashier had she delivered the gift while Baba was home during the day. Then Paige could have walked in, and voilà! Jillian could have switched on the power. As it was, unpacking was so time-consuming that Paige drifted off to work on dinner, and Baba started reading "Talk of the Town" in last week's *New Yorker*. With no outlet in reach, she had to ask for an extension cord, and lacking spares on hand Baba had to resort to a power strip whose disconnection would disable his stereo speakers.

At last, after Jillian had whisked around the floor filling three enormous black trash bags with Bubble Wrap, she tied her ribbon (alas, crumpled) around the trunk, and the moment was upon them. Baba called Paige away from her cutting board, and she returned to the living room, wiping her hands on a dish towel. Baba had helped Jillian position the lamp at its most becoming angle—though some rearrangement of furniture might be required in order to show off her creation to its best advantage and make it look at home here. She hit the switch.

"Well," Paige said. "That's really something, isn't it."

Baba seemed to take in the chandelier anew. When he said, "It's wonderful," he hit a note of wistfulness as well as awe, and the assertion didn't flush Jillian with quite the same heat as the first time he said that. But then, these infusions of perfect satisfaction don't necessarily come around more than once.

"Thank you," Paige said formally. "I'm sure no one else will give us a wedding present anything like yours. And it's always going to remind us of you, isn't it?"

As Jillian explained the derivation of a few elements, Paige's expression remained more polite than fascinated, and she cut the museum tour short. No one sat down. She was mildly surprised not to be asked to stay for a bite, though she'd arrived without warning, and maybe they had only two stuffed peppers or something. While that shouldn't have precluded a refresher of the wine, that glass must have been the end of a bottle. And sure, it wasn't a long walk back to the cottage; the summer evening was soft. Still, even if she'd have declined, it might have been nice to have at least been offered a ride home.

Y̲ou hate it." They had waited to speak until hearing Frisk crunch safely to the end of the gravel drive.

"I hate the fact of it," said Paige. "Though I'll grant it's not *quite* as ugly as I'd pictured."

"I don't know what we're going to do with it if you find it a torture."

"For now, we're not going to do anything," she said, U-turning briskly to the kitchen to resume chopping onions. "One upside of the long-term prospects for that friendship—meaning, it *has* no long-term prospects—is that after the wedding, we can do whatever we want with it, and she'll never know. In the meantime, on the off chance she comes back here again—unannounced, with the standard presumption—I guess we haven't any choice but to let that hulking contraption take up a third of our living room to keep from hurting her feelings."

It hit Weston then, the absurdity of protecting Frisk's

feelings for four more weeks, only to summarily crush them. The illogic recalled capital cases in which condemned men fell ill, and the state devoted all manner of expensive medical care to reviving convicts it planned to kill.

"I know you think she means well," Paige recommenced at dinner. "But it's so inappropriate! For a wedding present? For one thing, it's physically intrusive. It's huge. And I'd never seen it. She had no idea whether I'd like it."

"Most people like it," Weston mumbled.

"But anything that occupies that much space is an imposition."

"I realize how hard it is for you to take it this way, but that chandelier is important to her, and I'm sure it was hard for her to part with it. That was a lavish gift. Emotionally lavish."

"In which case, it's even more inappropriate. It's excessive, as usual. She has no business giving you an 'emotionally lavish' gift. What's wrong with a set of coasters?"

"That chandelier was a labor of love."

"A labor of love for herself! Those knickknacks glued every which way are all about *her*. A wedding present should be about us. Honestly, I no sooner begin to see the horizon beyond which we can stop fighting over that woman than she moves into our house. As a leering, beady-eyed monstrosity, peering at us while we eat. It's not any different than if Tracey Emin gave us her filthy bed. With used condoms, cigarette butts, and smears of menstrual blood on the sheets."

"Now it's not only Frisk who's going overboard. You can't equate a used condom with a toy whistle."

"I'm just having fun." Paige leaned over to kiss him, and the discussion was over—for tonight.

In retrospect, the expectation had been crazy. For three solid months, Weston would bop around the court with Frisk, interspersing chatty, musing dinners, in the full knowledge that at the knell of August twenty-sixth a curtain would drop on the whole relationship. In this loopy version of events, the friendship would still perk along as if nothing were the matter. Frisk would keep bearing down on that erratic but occasionally devastating crosscourt backhand. Weston would share his recipe for quick-pickling fresh vegetables in miso paste. And then one day—August twenty-*fifth*, say—it would be, Oh, by the way, we're never going to meet again, so long, it's been real.

In contrast to this fantasy, his treatment of Frisk all summer had been perfectly wretched. Unconsciously or otherwise, he'd been trying to gradually widen a distance between the two—just as you work a baby tooth loose with your tongue until it clings by a thread, making the extraction itself almost painless. Well, so much for the application of dentistry to human relations. He'd been subjecting Frisk to flat-out torture. Were his accelerating remoteness meant to make the imminent severance any less agonizing for himself, even there the technique had backfired. Acting like a prick had made him feel only worse, and for weeks, he'd done nothing but suffer.

An alternative to the working-the-baby-tooth model glared. What's less excruciating, inching into a cold swimming pool, or diving in? Peeling a Band-Aid slo-mo, or ripping it off? So why not get it over with?

Because he didn't want to. He didn't want to, he didn't have to yet, so he wouldn't.

Weston Babansky was a coward. He hadn't taken a bold, difficult decision in May; he'd taken half a decision. The easy half. Ever since the announcement to Paige that he would comply with her terms—ever since his sorrowful, downcast concession that he could see why no wife should be asked to tolerate another woman waiting in the wings, another confidante, an ex-lover of all things, and a rather intemperate one at that, who wasn't always artful about negotiating the spiky geometry of the triangle—day-to-day domestic life had certainly been more tranquil. The late-night scenes over his best friend had subsided. Paige was patient with his continuing to see Frisk on court, albeit with a tinge of triumphalism. He hated to think that she would take enjoyment in another woman's impending pain, though Weston had a bad habit of holding others to standards he wouldn't meet himself. Anyone would feel the frisson of victory on summarily trouncing a perceived rival.

A lifelong procrastinator, he'd been cashing in on the benefits of ditching Frisk while not paying the price. The hard part was the other half of the decision, which, being the hard part, was obviously the whole decision: telling Frisk. Because he had just enough wit to realize that, when you announce a relationship is going to be over, it is over right then.

The sole argument in his defense was that if he was trying to eat and have cake, it had not so long before been very good cake. Overoptimistic and idiotic, obviously, the aspiration was also tender: he'd hoped to safeguard one last summer with his favorite tennis partner.

Yet predictably, his fiancée's having articulated all that was wrong with the woman had made Weston more irritable with Frisk—which is to say, at all irritable—and more inclined to nitpick. That paean to Paige, for example, had been so strained, so conspicuously trying-too-hard, that he'd wanted to hit her. The unremitting corruption of her forehand (why ever would a player with a perfectly serviceable stroke suddenly install a fatal flip of the wrist—for *variety*?) actually moved him to rage, and expressing the fury as mere frustration required ungodly self-control. However curtailed their courtside debriefs, he found himself listening with a different ear: there she was, talking about herself again. When he told her about revisiting the National Gallery with Paige, her questions were flat, few, and generic. It must have been true, after all, that Frisk didn't really care for him, that she used him only as an audience.

It goaded him, too, how insensitive Frisk remained to the fact that Paige disliked her. Was his best friend dense? She'd had enough experience with detractors by now, so how could she still be so poorly attuned to positively semaphoric social cues? What did it take for Frisk to get the message? Did Paige have to march into the room wearing a T-shirt printed I HATE YOU? Physically attack her with a coal shovel?

In times past he'd have been endeared, yet even the billowy overkill of Bubble Wrap around the chandelier had been vexatious. Showing up at the A-frame out of the blue, staging a trashy striptease on the lawn, taking over the living room for an hour and a half, appealing to Paige for a bowled-over gratitude that would never be forthcoming . . . The whole production demonstrated Frisk's weird obliviousness to other people, her blindness to the fact that what they wanted might be contrary to what Frisk wanted. For Christ's sake, if she'd simply *asked* him whether he thought the lamp would make a suitable wedding present, he might have figured out a diplomatic way of fending the present off.

But here was the super weird thing: he was delighted to have it. Though Weston was not about to emphasize as much to Paige, he adored the Standing Chandelier, which melted him, and induced an emotional falling sensation, every time he laid eyes on it. Since the lamp had arrived in their possession, he had routinely basked in its glimmer for the long hours after Paige went to bed. Maybe Frisk did have a problem with alcohol, because something about the light it gave off went irresistibly with whiskey.

Obviously with a D-day looming, Weston was always going to find it a challenge to have a wonderful time while steeped in dread. Yet if his intention was to conduct a final halcyon season as a monument to all the bucolic seasons that went before it—to which he might later refer as a keepsake, raising his hands to the memory of the summer sun as he warmed himself at the woodstove, once an uncommonly lonely wintertime advanced—it made absolutely no sense, did it, to be mean to Frisk. Ironically, Frisk alone would have been able to understand that being mean to Frisk was one surefire method of being mean to himself. For it seemed that Weston had become the bad guy coming and going. He was a terrible person because he was unfaithful to his fiancée, and he was a terrible person because he was unfaithful to his best friend. Mooning over Talisker, Weston would suppose morosely that if he simply disappeared himself from this equation, both women would be fine. To retreat into self-pity was cowardly, but recall: he *was* a coward.

The better course for the month of August wasn't to stop feeling sorry for himself, but to start feeling sorry for the other parties, too. He had already to battle resentment in relation to the woman he was pledged to marry, which was no fit state in which to embark on a life together. But any expectation that Weston would accede to her wishes gladly was absurd. Cutting off the friendship with Frisk was bound to feel like cutting off his arm. Then again, the more sizable a sacrifice his fiancée appeared to be demanding, the more amply it was demonstrated that she was right to demand it.

As the reckoning neared, feeling sorry for Frisk came naturally. The way this scenario was playing out,

Weston and Paige would walk off into the sunset hand in hand. Frisk would be left with nothing—not even her most cherished possession, relinquishment of which Paige only held against her. (That said, several guests from William and Lee had been entranced by the lamp, as a consequence of which she had grown somewhat less hostile toward the object itself.) So partly as a reward for the chandelier, since it was the only reward that Frisk would reap, from the wedding present onward Weston was kind to her.

Too kind? He worried that his compassion was oppressive. Perhaps he was afflicting her with the same good intentions that must suffocate the terminally ill, whose friends and relatives continuously testify to the upstanding character of the dead-to-be. After the stink of all those flowers, the relentless puff of praise and pillow plumping, he wouldn't be surprised if cancer patients come to beg for the restorative of a harsh word.

For he would catch himself announcing, apropos of not much, that the hours spent with Frisk were "some of the most enjoyable of his life," or over-reassuring that despite the inexplicable disintegration of her forehand he "still loved playing with her more than anyone." She'd eye him suspiciously, wondering what his problem was. Theirs was a knockabout friendship, and they were supposed to be taking each other for granted.

"Do you ever wonder what it would have been like if you and I had made a go of it?" Frisk asked idly on the bench, a few days into the Month of Nauseating Niceness.

"Not really," Weston said quickly. She was making him anxious. "Dwelling on the counterfactual is a waste of energy."

"The *counterfactual!* Well, la-di-da. Maybe we'd have bombed because you have a rod up your ass."

"It doesn't bear thinking about," he reiterated firmly.

"Well, that's weird. And fancy-pants, too. *It doesn't bear thinking about.* As if you're afraid to think about it. And since when are you afraid to think about anything? I was only speculating. It's not as if I'm about to rip your clothes off or something."

He tucked the exchange away, as evidence that he had made the correct decision. There wasn't a great deal of evidence accumulating along these lines, so the encounter became strangely precious.

It was August fifteenth, a Wednesday. Considering that memories of their summer assignations tended to blur into one long, searing session, the fact that Weston would later recall the exact date would alone prove depressing. Frisk's demeanor was bubbly, as it had been ever since delivering her wedding present, which she appeared to believe had magically pressed a reset button. In Frisk's view, his warmer disposition was an effort to make up for having been churlish, crabby, and detached for months. She'd no doubt dismissed the dyspeptic humor as one more funk of the sort they'd survived for decades: arising from no cause, subsiding from no cure.

"I thought the Wrist Epilepsy wasn't so bad today," she announced.

"Yes, your forehand's been much more solid the last three or four times we've played," he said. This was true. That deadly flopping forward during her follow-through seemed to be a barometer of something, and he'd established this much: when he was mean to her, it got worse.

"Hey, I've been meaning to ask," she said. "This wedding-and-picnic thing. What's the dress code? Are we still supposed to ritz it up, with heels and flounces? Or is the idea more checkered tablecloth, and even jeans are fine?"

Weston focused on the rookies flailing on court no. 2, as if strokes better suited to badminton were terribly fascinating. "The concept is casual, but it is a wedding, so some women are likely to dress up."

"Well, what's Paige wearing? I gather you're not supposed to show up in anything that outshines the bride."

"You know her tastes." Squinting, he followed the incompetents' ball as it sailed over the fence, regretting that they hadn't hit it in this direction, so that he could fetch it for them. Anything to interrupt this line of inquiry. "Simple, no lace."

"I'm picturing a sleeveless sheaf, matte finish, all clean lines no trim, but with killer shoes."

The description was so astonishingly on target that for a moment he had to question whether Frisk really paid no attention to other people. "Something like that," he said vaguely.

"See, I was considering red, and I was worried about being too loud."

He turned to her. "Since when do you worry about being loud?"

She laughed. She didn't take the rejoinder the wrong way, and she should have.

"Also, I wanted to ask you about the food," she continued. "I assume your family coming from Wilmington, and Paige's from Baltimore, means they'll probably show up empty-handed, or at best bring, like, commercial pie. So I'd be happy to bring more than one thing. Either that, or I could make a serious quantity of something, because the problem with potluck is all these tiny dishes, and then everyone takes a timid tablespoon, and you end up with a plate that's incoherent—"

"We're having a barbecue," he cut her off.

"Oh!" she said, as if taken aback by his tone. About time, too. "I'm surprised you haven't mentioned that before. If you need someone to mind the coals, you know you can trust me not to burn the chicken."

"Paige's friends from the History Department are manning the grill."

Weston had moved on to looking riveted by a nondescript brown bird foraging in the crabgrass, thus keeping his gaze trained a good hundred degrees from his tennis partner's face. But he could tell she was peering at him.

"What about setup? I could help to put up tables, and lug cases of champagne—"

"All the bases are covered."

The fact that she hadn't pulled up short by now suggested experimental intent, as if she were delivering an escalating electrical shock to a lab rat and recording its response. "Still . . . It might be good to have, say, a carb—enough that everyone could have some? I told you about that Lebanese *freekeh* with roasted vegetables, which came out smashing. The recipe would be easy to multiply—"

"Frisk!" For this lab rat, the fibrillation had crossed a critical threshold. "You're not invited to the wedding! Why *else* you do you think you never got the email?"

He'd been afraid he would explode, and he had exploded.

That announcement had not been on the agenda for the afternoon.

Skipping even the clichéd incredulity of "*What?*" she dropped the boppy deportment cold. She was still and grave. "Why. Not."

"Paige doesn't like you." He hadn't intended to say that, either. He hadn't intended to say that, ever.

"Ah." She sat back on the bench. Her expression reminded Weston of doing a find-and-replace in a large Word file. There was a lag, and then a window popped up, 247 REPLACEMENTS MADE. "I've been having dinner with you guys for coming up on three years. You'd think I would have noticed."

"Yes, well. I've been surprised you haven't."

"Here I was thinking your girlfriend and I got on pretty well."

"I think it's a chemistry thing," he said, unsure whether the irremediable nature of chemistry made it better or worse.

"Is it?" He might have expected her to cry, but instead she was cool and clear. Unsettlingly composed, in fact. "Something inexpressible, then. Nothing she could put her finger on."

"Sort of," he said glumly.

"So she wouldn't have cited any of her problems with me in particular."

"Oh . . . She has mentioned your being, well, a little showy, a little self-involved. You know, her whole style is lower profile and more self-effacing. But I don't see what's to be gained from going into any detail. It would just hurt your feelings."

"No, we wouldn't want to do *that*."

They sat.

"I can only infer," she resumed, "that this 'dislike' goes back a ways?"

"She's felt uncomfortable around you for a while, yeah."

"So you and I have been chatting after tennis for years, and you've never said a word about Paige being 'uncomfortable.'"

"It's not nice, is it? I don't even think I should have told you just now."

"Because you and I only tell each other nice things."

"We tell each other what's helpful, or try to."

"We used to tell each other the truth. And now we've gone this whole summer, you sitting there knowing I'm not welcome at your wedding, and letting me prattle on about what to wear."

"I'm sorry. I was putting off telling you, obviously. This isn't easy for me, either."

"This *discomfort*, which I hadn't realized before is a synonym for *loathing*—it's not only because I'm too colorful for quiet, unassuming Paige, is it? I mean, it wouldn't have anything to do with *jealousy*, would it?"

"You could call it that."

"Good. Let's call it that."

He'd never have expected her to be so icy. "She finds you a little possessive. Of me."

"I do possess you. In my way. Or I used to."

"Then you can see why that might be difficult for her."

"No, I can't. She possesses you, too, in a different way. I don't see why there's a conflict."

"You usually have a more nuanced sense of how people work."

"Here's my nuance: if she trusts you—and if she doesn't, she has no business marrying you—then she should be cool with inviting your best friend to your wedding, even if I'm not her favorite person in the world. Since I assume everyone else on the guest list hasn't been vetted for being too 'showy' or 'self-involved.'"

When Paige had laid out her case, the just course seemed so clear. Weston had to stop himself from clapping his hands over his ears. "That's the way it seems to you."

"Of course it 'seems that way to me'; that's why I'm the one who's saying it. But it also *seems to me* that this situation is a great deal more complicated than my now being free to make other plans for August twenty-sixth. It's not just that I've been absolved of any requirement to make a big vat of *freekeh* beforehand. Because if I'm not invited to your wedding"—she leaned forward—"*what else am I not invited to?*"

Weston pressed the pads of his fingers to his forehead, now granular with salt. *My life*, he thought. *You are no longer invited to my whole life.* She'd been his best friend cum beloved tennis partner for a quarter century, and she was right. He owed her the truth.

It might have been tasteless or insensitive, but pure force of habit moved him to say when they parted, "See you on Friday." Yet he'd actually been planning to play with her, too, as he would also have shown up at Rockbridge County High School with his racket, water, sweatband, and a new can of Wilsons on the twentieth, twenty-second, and twenty-fourth the following week. All summer, he had clung to Paige's permission that he could run out the season with Frisk until August twenty-sixth, and it was merely the fifteenth. Only when Frisk stared and said, "Have you lost your mind?" was the new order real to him, as it would be even more so on Friday—sleeping feverishly into the late afternoon because there was no four p.m. tennis date for which to wake.

By the following summer, Jillian had found three other people to hit with in a rotation every week, and the variety was probably better for her game. But she was surprised to discover that she didn't care about her game. She kept up the sport to get relatively painless exercise, but tennis as she had once conceived it—the soul of the present tense, the one activity that from moment to moment was exactly what she wanted to be doing and nothing else, a pure kinetic joy—had long been synonymous with her friendship with Baba, and playing with anyone else wasn't the same.

At least seeing the three poor substitutes put her in contact with a handful of other adults besides the parents of her students. For a long time after the breakup—she didn't think you were supposed to "break up" with friends, but she didn't know what else to call it—she avoided people.

She could no longer trust her own judgment. Competent animals could sniff out threat. They instinctively distinguished their own kind, and anodyne adjacent wildlife, from predators. So it was in the spirit of biological imperative that she reviewed her many intersections with Paige Myer. Their first meeting: That hadn't been a slightly inept young woman with a tendency to blurt her fiercely held convictions. It was an outburst of immediate, uncontrollable aversion of a kind Jillian should have recognized. Because Paige would already have heard as much about Jillian as Jillian had heard about her, chances were high that Paige had *prehated* her, much as one preorders a book, or a burial plot. Some characters might be so beguiling on introduction that they are able to penetrate a shield of prepared enmity with the sword of their fearsome charm, but examples of prevailing against prehatred are probably few.

Thereafter: Paige wasn't bashful, and she wasn't quiet. She was subdued around Jillian because that's what people were like when the whole night through they were shoving a fist in their mouths and waiting for a guest to leave.

The presents (the shawl, the fig preserves): camouflage.

Various admirations (of the necklaces, the button self-portrait, even the high-loft popcorn): fake. Jillian made a note to self: she was as big a pushover for flattery as every other bozo.

Jillian's respectful efforts to act more formal with Weston Babansky in Paige's presence: wasted. Read as patronizing. Though it wouldn't have helped had she acted in another manner instead, as any alternative approach would have backfired, too.

The point was, if Jillian Frisk couldn't tell the difference between a shy, diffident, openhanded new acquaintance and a nemesis gunning for her most precious asset from the get-go, she shouldn't be allowed out in public.

The near agoraphobia following that awful August was aggravated by a still more pernicious mistrust. Launching into the outside world requires feeling faintly palatable. At the least, in social settings you have to adopt the default assumption that others' initial reaction to you will be neutral, and healthy characters walk into a room expecting to be actively liked. But for months, Jillian felt hateable. Lest she appear "showy," she dressed in small colors, wearing slack T-shirts and tired jeans that disguised her figure. She kept her hair bunched, and often skipped showers so that its tendrils wilted. Lest she seem "self-involved," she conducted all phone calls with such a paucity of autobiographical content that her mother in Philadelphia accused her of being secretive. When she met the disappointing tennis partners, she volunteered little enough about her off-court life that they stopped asking, and consigned the relationship to the sports friendship, a perfectly agreeable but utilitarian arrangement whereby you never saw one another other than to play. In general, Jillian tried to say and do as little as possible, because whatever she expressed and however she behaved was bound to inspire disgust.

Mind, one of the primary reasons most people dislike someone is that the other party doesn't like *them*; thus so many antagonisms come down to a chicken-and-egg issue of who started it. Yet Jillian found Paige Myer strangely difficult to despise in return. There simply wasn't that much prospectively odious material to work with. Baba's renunciation naturally feeling like a betrayal, Jillian might have taken refuge in right-eous indignation—alas, a deflective, huffy emotion, in this case hopelessly subsumed by sheer woundedness. She couldn't hate him, either, which would only pile betrayal upon betrayal. You were supposed to love a wife more than a pal, right? So it made sense that Baba had thrown their friendship under a bus, the way earlier generations of gallants threw capes over puddles.

Consuming the better part of a year, her bereavement was so deep and enduring that she might have wondered whether, as Baba had insinuated that dreadful Wednesday, the undercurrents of the friendship were indeed improper. Except that no romance had wrecked her this thoroughly for this long, regardless of how besotted she'd been to begin with. In the end, the unique severity of the loss seemed to exonerate their amity as innocent after all.

Inevitably, she would catch sight of him. He did give their old courts wide berth; it was tacitly understood that she'd been awarded Rockbridge, as if having been bequeathed no. 3 in a divorce settlement. But downtown Lexington was tiny, its eateries few. The first time she spotted Baba coming out of Macado's on Main Street, she ran away, cowering around the corner on West Henry. Not an adult response. She got better at fielding these intersections, nodding from down the block if she caught his eye, sometimes cracking a despondent half smile. He was always the one who broke the gaze first to look down at the sidewalk. Then he'd glance back up and flutter a lifeless wave, having trouble raising his hand, as if the once keen sportsman had contracted some terrible muscle-wasting disease. On each sighting, he looked thinner—unattractively so. All that vegetarianism.

By late spring, however, Jillian started to feel hardier, and reconsidered the plan she'd conceived over the winter to pick up stakes. She had a sweet arrangement with the Chevaliers that she was unlikely to duplicate elsewhere. She loved her cottage, its floors refinished with darker lines patterning the edges of the rooms like tribal tattoos. Her reputation as a lively, infectiously enthusiastic tutor had spread widely enough—to nearby Kerrs Creek, Mechanicsville, and Buena Vista—that she didn't want for work, even if her secret with the boys was that most of them developed crushes. It was a comely, close-knit municipality that she had made her home, and on the face of it, the rejection of a tennis partner was a lunatic reason to leave town.

As the weather warmed and her skin turned golden, she began to feel braver, donning more revealing skirts and the flouncy thrift shop tops she had shunned for months. She went back to wearing hats—wide brimmed, straw, with ribbons. She let her hair down in every sense, and kept it washed. She rediscovered that a broad grin in Sweet Things Ice Cream Shoppe was all it took to win an extra-generous scoop and free sprinkles. A widowed client raising two sons, who by the by was rather dishy, had started asking her to stick around after lessons for a glass of wine. The only individual in her orbit who appeared to find her "hateable" was Jillian herself. So she tried the Ice Cream Shoppe smile in her bedroom mirror, and the reflection smiled right back.

Whether she precisely forgave Baba—whom she was starting to think of as *Weston*—was a moot point. The purpose of forgiveness was to lay planks over a gorge in the interest of forging ahead, and instead her erstwhile soul mate had raised one of those stark black-and-yellow END signs meant to alert motorists to the termination of a cul-de-sac. How she felt about Paige, likewise never again actively germane to Jillian's affairs, was equally irrelevant. Although forevermore a particular place in her mind was destined to ache when she brushed against it, she was apparently capable of moving on.

But as the loss of her best friend gradually healed over, another hole in her life continued to gape.

The back right quarter of her living room was empty. She had never chosen to rebalance the room by returning the armchair there. What was done was done: *Weston* had forsaken their friendship to appease his wife. But one injustice could be righted.

On the exact date at the end of July marking the one-year anniversary of a big mistake, Jillian wrote the following email:

Dear Weston,

I hope you don't mind my contacting you this way.
While I do miss you sometimes, I am well, and I am
not trying to stir up trouble. I trust that you and Paige
are very happy.

A year ago, I gave you and your fiancée a wedding
present that cost me a great deal of time, energy, and
love. The materials I used to construct it, like my own
wisdom teeth, are irreplaceable. So it was very difficult
for me to give away my handiwork—which was literally
imbued with my own DNA. Had things gone differently
between the three of us, however, rest assured that I
would still be delighted to have given my creation a new
home, where I could be certain it would be cherished.

As it happens, you accepted the gift under false
pretenses. The evening I bestowed it, you were already
planning to bring our friendship to a permanent close.
You were also keenly aware that your wife-to-be
disliked me, a fact that you concealed from me,
allowing me to make a fool of myself by proceeding
as if she and I had warm, harmonious relations. Had I
benefited from access to both these pieces of
information at the time, I would never have given you

the Standing Chandelier—of which I am now not only dispossessed, but which I can't even visit.

I would like it back. I don't mean to be an Indian giver. (Paige wouldn't approve; I think that expression is no longer PC, though I don't know of another expression that has replaced it.) We could arrange an exchange, just as many newlyweds take their ugly ceramic cheese boards back to Pottery Barn and trade them for store credit. I'll replace the chandelier with a set of nice wine-glasses or something, and then you can break them.

In any case, I can't imagine Paige treasures a reminder of someone she detests. I would even think that an inti-mate memento of our long but cruelly truncated friendship would be painful for you also. I would be glad to come by to pick it up when neither of you are home. Perhaps you could leave a key and instructions with a neighbor. I would even bring the bubble wrap.

Yours sincerely,
Jillian Frisk

"That is so completely lacking in class," Paige announced over Weston's computer in the A-frame's second-floor alcove. It was before dinner in early August. "Okay, sure, once in a while a wedding is called off. Then, yes, a couple with any integrity returns the presents—voluntarily, I might add. But I've never in my life heard of anyone giving a wedding present and then demanding it *back*."

"It's a little more complicated than that, isn't it?" Weston said tentatively.

"It is not. You always want to make everything out as complicated. This is straightforward. It's crass."

"While she obviously tried to write that email politely, I agree that the request itself is a little spiteful. So what do you want to do? Knowing she begrudges our having it—I don't know how I'd feel about keeping that thing."

Paige gave him an affectionate poke. "You never know how you feel. Maybe we could consult a year from now and take a barometric reading of the Babansky soul."

She was right. He functioned on emotional hold, operating a more protracted version of the seven-second delay on radio broadcasts to check for Federal Communications Commission obscenity no-nos. He had put off showing Paige the email for the last three days, because his own reaction to it was so undiscernibly mixed—a sludge of dread, sorrow, and irritation.

"One thing I don't understand," Paige added. "If she was going to be so gauche, what took her so long? It's been a year."

"Maybe it took her a while to figure out what she felt, too."

"That's generous. As usual, given the subject matter. I would have hoped she's just been getting on with her life, but clearly she's been stewing this whole time. Writing that same email over and over in her mind. And even so, she can't control herself! That line about how she could give us some glasses instead, 'and then we could break them.' The bitterness, it's like having a double espresso thrown in your face, no sugar."

The bitterness was two-way. Paige herself was sounding a note he hadn't heard since the previous summer. She was not in the main given to recrimination or viciousness. The only topic that drew these qualities from Paige was Jillian Frisk. Best let his wife get the vitriol out of her system, then. Maybe he should be positively grateful for having obtained such a home remedy. The subject of his old friend could extract the residual traces of rancor from his wife's character like a poultice.

"And you said she was polite. But the cordiality is fraudulent," she carried on, having bent again over his computer. "'I trust that you and Paige are very happy,'" she read in a mincing tone. "Notice she can't resist getting in a dig at me with that crack about not being 'PC,' when what she really means is that she's a cultural troglodyte. Because she's right, you're not supposed to say 'Indian giver' anymore, as if anyone should ever have said it in the first place. And when you realize that, you don't *write* 'Indian giver,' you write something else. Oh, and I like her saying she doesn't 'mean to be' an Indian giver, when that's exactly what she's being."

Now was not the time to observe that Paige had just used the very expression that she claimed to deplore. He found it mysterious that she still got so worked up over Frisk, whom she had vanquished in every way. He'd have thought she would feel a touch of pity, or nothing.

"Oh, and notice how it's *your* fault that she 'made a fool of herself,'" Paige went on. "Just because she's socially oblivious and never picked up that she got on my nerves. The melodrama, too! Your 'cruelly truncated friendship.' And I have to 'detest' her. It's not just that Jillian isn't my cup of tea."

This email forensic was curiously heavy on beverages. "Well," Weston allowed. "You did say you 'couldn't stand her when you met her' and you 'couldn't stand her when you got to know her better' either. I'm not sure what you call that but detesting someone."

"I can't believe you can quote word for word something I said that long ago."

"It was memorable."

"Detestation—if that's the noun—is a feeling that eats you up. So it's hardly pertinent to someone I never think about."

*Uh-huh*, Weston stifled. "I know I said I wouldn't communicate with her. But even if you find the email overwritten, or inaccurate about your feelings, I think it deserves a reply. That's why I showed it to you. So we could decide what to say."

"Of course you showed it to me. I'd be alarmed if you didn't. You haven't been corresponding with her all along, have you? And are only showing me this one because it involves us both?"

"We haven't been corresponding," Weston said flatly. He might have gone on at greater length, either in umbrage or with fervid reassurance, but amid the range of emotions he battled whenever Frisk arose in their discussions the most dominant was exhaustion, and he kept the denial short. "The point is, she wants the lamp back. So I guess we should let her have it."

"You must be kidding! It was a *wedding present*!"

"I thought you didn't like the chandelier anyway."

"I don't like calling it a 'chandelier'—that part is true. It's not a 'chandelier,' which is a pompous, totally inane thing to call a *lamp*. Still, even if it's not entirely to my taste, it's grown on me. Or at least I've gotten used to it. And we rearranged the whole living room to accommodate that thing."

In truth, Frisk's addition to their household cornerstoned the decor of the whole ground floor. It was a great conversation starter with new dinner guests, who often exceeded exuberant enthusiasm to confess to outright envy. Bill from the History Department had gleefully rechristened it "The

Memory Palace," a branding he seemed to believe was sparklingly original; having contrived a new name also encouraged the guy to act weirdly proprietary, as if he were a museum director and this artwork was only resting in their living room on loan. The light the lamp cast was uniquely soft, enclosing, and warm, and Weston couldn't imagine ever finding a proxy that would duplicate these qualities in a world of glaring compact fluorescents. He still routinely worked beside it during the wee smalls in his regular rocking chair, the radiance emitting from the windows of the Colman's mustard tin mingling with the glow of his computer. In all honesty, the object reminded him less and less of Frisk; he was now capable of spending whole hours in its presence without her crossing his mind even once.

Catching himself in this admission moved him to remind Paige, "But this isn't about a thing. It's about what it means. Frisk really put her heart into that—" He was about to say *chandelier*, and thought better of it. "So for her, it's symbolic of, well, giving her heart. Which we sort of stepped on, or that's how she would see it."

"Is that the way you see it?"

"It's just, I'm getting the impression you definitely don't want to give it back."

"Better believe it."

"Which would seem, to Frisk, like stepping on her heart twice."

"The symbolism? That present is symbolic of Jillian for once in her life doing the traditional, decent thing and giving an acquaintance of long standing a wedding present— even if the present itself was a little weird. For us to acquiesce and let her snatch it back would be to say, yet again, that the rules governing everyone else don't apply to her, and she can behave as badly as she likes and get whatever she wants, other people be damned."

Weston let *acquaintance* slide. "You didn't say at the time it was 'a little weird.' You called it 'inappropriate' and 'an imposition' and 'a beady-eyed monstrosity.' You compared it to Tracey Emin's bed."

"You're doing that again. Quoting me verbatim from last summer. What, did you run off and take notes, so you could hang me with them later?"

"If that lamp is symbolic of anything, it's symbolic of my friendship with Frisk. Because she's right on one point: it's always going to remind you of her. So why on earth would you want to hang on to it?"

"Because it distresses me that all this time later, with one lousy go-fetch email, you'll still do her bidding. Which makes me wonder."

"Don't *wonder*," he said with annoyance. He was no

longer wondering himself. *That lamp doesn't only remind my wife of her adversary. It reminds her of winning.* "But what on earth can I write back?"

"I could draft that email in a heartbeat. 'Dear Jillian: What you're asking goes so beyond the limits of decorum that it's off the charts. A wedding present is forever, just like my marriage. Have a nice life.'"

"I guess I'll have to think about it."

Her laughter had an unpleasant color. "What a shock."

Weston had not replaced Frisk—or, to the degree that he had, he had replaced her with Paige. The confidences, the day-to-day anecdotes, the many ambivalences with which he wrestled, even the recipes, successful and disappointing alike, he shared with his wife. That was as it should be, he supposed. As a consequence of this substitution—this wife swap, if you will—it was possible that some small slice of himself was stifled. But that's what solitude was for: exploring the unsayable. He was becoming one of those commonplace men whose sole intimacy was with a spouse, while friendship, exclusively with other men, was reserved for talk about movies and football. Except that Weston wasn't interested in football.

He was still interested in tennis, and had finally joined

the local club, which he could now afford. His partners there were male, and they always played formal matches. He was rising on the ladder. No longer merely rallying with Frisk three times a week, he'd improved his serve.

It had not been optimal to begin his marriage in a spirit of sacrifice. But he had instructed himself on the necessity of the Frisk forfeiture enough times to begin to believe it. On reflection, Paige's request had been so justified, its reasoning so solid, that it was astonishing earlier girlfriends hadn't laid down the same law. (Some of his wife's romantic predecessors had also found the Frisk situation fishy, but they'd kept the grumbling to a minimum. Either they hadn't loved him enough to put up a stink, or they knew he didn't love them enough to capitulate.) Weston being Weston, he had naturally examined the question of whether he should feel guilty about Frisk from every angle. The answer was no. Human relations had a calculus, and sometimes you had to add up columns of gains and losses with the coldness of accountancy. He was a happier man married. Although he would eternally suffer from funks, they were fewer and shorter now. He was glad to have put to rest a quest that would otherwise fester—biology ensured that—and to have escaped the fate of men forever single into their fifties, who reliably earned reputations as strange, gay, emotionally dislocated, or all three. Settledness suited him. Only women were meant to care about safety, but safety was a universally appealing state, and men could snug into it, too. He enjoyed the regular rhythms of his days with Paige, like the rise and fall of swells on a coastal vacation. During his boyhood in Wilmington, an hour's drive from the Jersey shore, Weston had spent many tireless hours lulled up and down beyond the breakers. If the cost of installing this sensation in his inland adulthood was doing without an alternative rhythm three times a week, so be it.

After they'd rehashed the *Indian giving* yet again after dinner and Paige had gone to bed, he poured himself a double Talisker and switched on the chandelier. He was frankly surprised that Frisk had brought herself to rescind the gift, because Paige was right: it wasn't classy. You'd think Frisk would have restrained herself, if only out of pride.

Yet after a few sips of whisky, the explanation fell into place. Pride was predominantly a social construct, having to do with witness. And why would Frisk fear his contempt for making an appeal that was beneath her? Aside from those few torturous bumpings into each other downtown—more like hauntings, or disquietingly vivid memories, than proper encounters—Weston played so little a part in her life now that he might have been dead. As for her own witness of this mean-spiritedness, which might invite regret: however inevitable their parting of ways, even Weston couldn't persuade himself that Frisk deserved his desertion. Whether or not the friendship was unacceptably tinged by mutual attraction, she'd never actually tried to kiss him again, had she? She hadn't tried to lure him back to bed. Not once convicted of a moving violation, she hadn't, strictly speaking, done anything wrong. Yet she had been roundly punished. So for Frisk, any passing private chagrin over *Indian giving* was bound to be swallowed by a far greater sense of grievance. Or grief? Idly, he checked the etymologies online. Both *grievance* and *grief* derived from the Old French *grever*, "to burden." That was about the sum of it. He had burdened her.

To resume: you obeyed conventions because you cared what other people thought of you. If Frisk and Weston were no longer friends, then Frisk had no cause to care what he thought of her. She'd have been well aware that the revocation of a wedding present was crass. So? His repudiation of their friendship had freed her from the bonds of seemliness. She had no reason to avoid asking something embarrassing, or even reason to feel embarrassed. For embarrassment as well was a social construct. Without relationship, there is no society. The ties between the two parties had been severed. All that remained was stuff. Thus she had nothing to lose by savaging his good opinion of her, and one thing to gain: her chandelier.

Here in this living room, the same paradigm repeated. Neither he nor Paige retained an investment in what Jillian Frisk thought of them. Plausibly, the only faux pas more crass than demanding the return of a wedding present was having a nuptial gift rudely retracted and refusing to give it back. So? They had nothing to gain by remaining theoretically in Frisk's good graces, and one thing to lose: the chandelier.

Structurally, then, a single disparity distinguished the two squared-off factions: he and Paige had custody of the item at issue, and Frisk didn't.

Were he to return the gift, he would do so over his wife's dead body. What was in it for him, taking all that flack, when at best he'd receive a single thank-you in his inbox as compensation? And Weston liked the chandelier, even liked calling it that, if it might take Paige a few more years to warm to the tag. The grand, eccentric centerpiece had already grown into the very being of the A-frame, as if the trunk of the lamp had extended roots through the oak flooring that were penetrating the ceiling of the utility room and gnarling around the pipes. Secreting its many objets d'art, miniature dioramas, and natural wonders like the curlew skull, the arboreal assemblage gave off enough hint of Yuletide to evoke the ringing refrain *And a partridge in a pear tree*. Squirm as she might to avoid admitting as much, Paige liked the chandelier, too—liked it very much, in fact, and she would come to like it more and more as the years advanced.

The lamp wasn't a symbol. All the meaning had been sucked out of it the afternoon he sank back onto their regular bench at Rockbridge to deliver the bad news, its limp elucidation taking so much less time than the rambling rationalizations of his rehearsals. They would all three continue to pretend that the chandelier was a symbol, when really it had become a thing. Frisk wanted the thing. Weston wanted the thing. Improbably, even Paige wanted the thing. A thing of which possession was ten-tenths, like most of one's belongings.

The Talisker was finished. At last Weston composed the shortest email he could muster:

Have discussed. Paige finds request violates social custom. Will continue to enjoy chandelier.

He'd signed it "B." to begin with, then changed that to "W.," couldn't bear the W, and didn't sign it at all.

Though he sent it at past three a.m., the response was immediate:

She just wants to keep her *scalp*.

He'd promised, and this was bordering on *correspondence*. After deleting not only Frisk's reply but also its ghost in TRASH, he swiftly closed the computer like the lid of Pandora's box.